HOPE HAS TWO DAUGHTERS

Also by Monia Mazigh

Fiction
Mirrors and Mirages

Nonfiction
Hope and Despair:
My Struggle to Free My Husband, Maher Arar

HOPE HAS TWO DAUGHTERS

MONIA MAZIGH

Translated by Fred A. Reed

ARACHNIDE

First published as *Du pain et jasmin* in 2015 by Les Éditions David
First published in English in 2017 by House of Anansi Press Inc.
www.houseofanansi.com

21 20 19 18 17   1 2 3 4 5

Library and Archives Canada Cataloguing in Publication

Mazigh, Monia
[Du pain et du jasmin. English]
Hope has two daughters / Monia Mazigh ; Fred A. Reed, translator.

Translation of: Du pain et du jasmin.
Issued in print and electronic formats.
ISBN 978-1-4870-0180-3 (paperback).—ISBN 978-1-4870-0181-0 (html)

1. Tunisia—History—Demonstrations, 2010- —Fiction. I. Reed, Fred
A., 1939-, translator II. Title. III. Title: Du pain et du jasmin. English.

PS8626.A955D813 2017   C843'.6   C2016-903814-9
                              C2016-903815-7

Library of Congress Control Number: 2016955869

Book design: Alysia Shewchuk

 Canada Council Conseil des Arts
for the Arts du Canada

 ONTARIO ARTS COUNCIL
CONSEIL DES ARTS DE L'ONTARIO
an Ontario government agency
un organisme du gouvernement de l'Ontario

We acknowledge for their financial support of our publishing program
the Canada Council for the Arts, the Ontario Arts Council, and the Government of Canada
through the Canada Book Fund. We acknowledge the financial support of the Government
of Canada, through the National Translation Program for Book Publishing, an initiative
of the Roadmap for Canada's Official Languages 2013–2018: Education, Immigration,
Communities, for our translation activities.

Printed and bound in Canada

 MIX
Paper from
responsible sources
FSC® C004071

AUTHOR'S NOTE

This book is a work of fiction, not an autobiography. Naturally, I have drawn on my childhood memories, but the characters in this story exist only in my imagination. The "bread riots," which were also called the "couscous revolt," did take place in Tunisia in 1984, as did the uprising of 2010–11 that led to the fall of the Ben Ali regime. Even though the novel's description of these events may suggest historical facts, the dates that appear here have been slightly modified to serve the needs of the story.

ONE

Tunis, January 3, 1984

I SAT THERE GRIMACING in pain, legs splayed, butt glued to the toilet seat. Sharp cramps stabbed my bowels with clockwork precision. A stinking torrent of diarrhea gushed out of me like super-heated water from a geyser, bringing sudden relief from the intense pain I'd been suffering minutes before. I felt better already. I looked around me and out underneath the wooden door with the peeling paint. The restroom was filthy — the tile floor was the colour of the mud that had been tracked in by the restaurant customers. I heard steps in the cubicle next to mine, followed by a loud hiss of urine that seemed unending. Then came a whoosh as the toilet flushed. I sat there motionless, ashamed; I couldn't get up; I didn't want anyone to see me. I had no idea what exactly had happened. I'd stopped off for a *keftaji* at this greasy spoon. But before I'd swallowed the last mouthful my bowels were growling so loud you could hear them. Violent cramps convulsed my whole body. I barely made it in time.

My day had gotten off to a very bad start. Around noon I was so hungry I could hardly see straight. Usually, I would bring a sandwich to eat when I met Neila. The two of us would sit atop the wall just in front of the fence, not far from the library of the *lycée,* and swing our legs back and forth like little girls practicing for some balancing act. Behind us, the ancient eucalyptus sheltered us in their generous shade. Their majestic branches bowed toward the ground.

Mother made me a sandwich every morning. She cut off a piece of the baguette she'd bought earlier at Hassan's, the neighbourhood grocer. Then she would slice it lengthwise, smear on a spoonful of *harissa* diluted with a bit of water, add a few morsels of tuna or a sardine, depending on whether it was the first or the last of the month, and top the whole thing off with a few drops of soya oil. My father hadn't been able to afford olive oil for several years now. The cost of living kept going up and up and his meagre salary as a clerk at the justice ministry couldn't keep pace. The first of every month was a bit of a festival for us. Father would buy cans of tuna.

"It's Sidi-Daoud, the best!" he would repeat, as though he was afraid we'd forgotten. Then he added:

"Sidi-Daoud is where the big Mediterranean bluefin tuna come to gorge themselves on tasty algae. That makes their meat appetizing and sweet smelling and it's right then that they're caught. *Mattanza*, the Italians call it..." Nobody paid attention to Father. We'd all learned his words by heart. The festivities would continue for a week or two; mother would prepare tuna and egg *briks*, and sprinkle a few flakes on the *mechouia*, the salad she made from tomatoes and charcoal-grilled red peppers.

But by month's end the money would have all but run out. The tension in the house was thick. That's when mother began doing the shopping, while father sat in his armchair directly in front of the TV. I knew he wasn't watching; he was worrying. Mother stopped buying meat; we simply couldn't afford it. That meant a strict vegetarian diet: chickpea soup, couscous with squash, spinach, and potatoes, pasta with beans, lentils and green peas. Talk about hard-luck cooking! For my daily sandwich she bought tins of insipid sardines packed in curious-tasting oil, nothing to compare with the tuna from Sidi-Daoud. But if I opened my mouth to complain or make a smart remark I was in trouble. Not a word! If I said something without a good reason, father would glare at me and mother would wag her finger under my nose, and the whole thing would end in a shouting match between them. I ate my fill in silence.

Recently there had been troubles in the south, which father had mentioned in passing. This seemed to add to the feeling of scarcity that had spread to Tunis and to our family home. Not that the situation interested me terribly. Trying to live my life was enough.

That morning mother had gone out early. I had no idea where. Shopping maybe, or to drop in to see our neighbour Hedia, little Najwa's mother. Hedia had just lost her husband. I was too lazy to fix myself anything, so I grabbed my things and headed off for school without bringing a lunch.

Neila didn't come to school that day. That morning I'd waited for her in front of her place, at the usual spot — the weed patch under the lamppost with the broken bulb — but she never showed up. She had seemed a bit tired when we parted in front of her building the day before, but she hadn't said anything.

Hopefully her father hadn't made one of his scenes again. The truth was that Mr. Abdelkader would beat his children for no reason. Nobody could stop him. He would let loose and go into full fury like the first rains of autumn, the ones we call *Ghassalat el-Nouader*, which means the mill-wheel washer. It was a powerful, driving rain that carried everything with it: heaps of gravel, piles of garbage, yellowed newspapers, and dead cats from vacant lots. Water poured from the sky with such force that the sewers would overflow, backing up water into residential neighbourhoods where rushing streams began to run. Fat raindrops dissolved the dust heaped up by summer's sirocco. It was like the *ghula* stories of our childhood innocence. When the torrent finally ended, people ventured out into the flooded streets to survey the damage.

I imagined Neila, looking in her mirror at the bruises on her body; I could see the tears rolling down her cheeks. Neila hated her father, hated his fits of rage against her and her brothers. She wanted to get out, to leave home, to never come back. She didn't want to end up like her mother, sunk deep in silence. Helpless to stop the oncoming storm. She'd brought it up a week ago.

"One of these days, I'll run away with Mounir. Then he'll see, the brute. He calls himself a father? Let him go croak all alone."

"What about your mother?" I asked. "You're going to leave her with him?"

Neila paid no attention to my words and fled my interrogator's gaze. Quickly she changed the subject. From the corner of my eye I could see her jaw moving rapidly back and forth. That was the sign that she'd lost her temper.

I PULLED UP my trousers, buckled my belt, adjusted my tunic, and, doing my best to appear invisible, slipped furtively from the filthy restroom. Fortunately no one saw me, and I felt relieved. My bellyache was gone. All I wanted was to get out of that stinking hole as fast as my feet would carry me. *I'll never set foot in here again*, I told myself over and over. I glanced at my watch: class would begin in a few minutes, so I picked up the pace. If I missed the first few minutes, I wouldn't be able to understand a thing.

By the time I entered the classroom, the instructor, Monsieur Kamel, was already at his desk, pulling thick file folders from his scuffed leather briefcase. Sonia was standing at the front of the class, and as usual, she was making eyes at him. She brushed back a thick strand of blond hair that had fallen over her eyes. Her ample breasts almost touched the edge of his desk. Monsieur Kamel looked ill at ease, and he was answering Sonia's questions like an automaton. I pulled my things from my school bag and glanced at the two of them out of the corner of my eye. From time to time, Monsieur Kamel's tiny round eyes came to rest on Sonia's breasts. At the rear of the classroom, the boys were sniggering viciously. I heard one of them utter an obscenity; then came an outburst of laughter followed by more sniggering. Meanwhile, Sonia kept at it. She wanted to get a passing grade; that much was clear. The whole class knew it except for Monsieur Kamel, who pretended not to notice a thing. I sat down at my usual place, by the window. Neila wasn't in class. Shivers ran up and down my spine. I could see her father's face, and it made my blood run cold. I imagined him, brows knotted, mouth twisted with rage, as he battered Neila's slender body. "Oh Lord, please let nothing terrible have happened!" I murmured to myself. To disperse the dark thoughts that were spinning in my mind, I decided that I would visit her on my way home from school.

At last Sonia returned to her seat, and Monsieur Kamel's eyes softened. Sonia was all but waggling her behind; her jeans looked as if they were about to split, to reveal her milky skin. But I couldn't forget Neila.

I was taking notes, my head down. Monsieur Kamel, hands thrust into his pockets, was speaking at top speed. Sonia was sucking the end of her pen as she toyed with her curls with her free hand. Monsieur Kamel stood up from his desk without interrupting his lecture. I wrote frantically, not wanting to miss a single word. Everything had to be written down, memorized, and then regurgitated at the proper moment for the final exam. I knew the method. I hated it, but I applied it to a T. My pen glided smoothly over the blank pages. Words and sentences filled my ears and congregated like moths drawn to the light, only to be driven away by a wild animal or imminent danger. Monsieur Kamel was making his way up and down the aisles between the desks, shoes shuffling across the floor. When he approached Sonia's desk his pace slowed. I thought I saw his hand brush Sonia's leg. From the back of the classroom, someone grunted loudly. Monsieur Kamel spun around. His face was flushed, his nostrils flared and sweat dripped from his forehead.

"Who's snorting like an ass?" he shouted. "What is this, an Arabic class or a zoo?"

A muffled laugh came from the back of the class-room. Monsieur Kamel was furious.

"You there, in the back, to the right, stand up. I don't want to see your face for the rest of the lesson."

Monsieur Kamel's fury was directed at Riad, a shy boy with a stutter. We never heard him talk, let alone laugh. Why had Monsieur Kamel picked on him? Red faced, lips pursed, Riad calmly picked up his things. He was not about to challenge the professor's verdict. I turned around to get a better look. How distant the rear of the classroom seemed! Head bowed, Riad made his way to the door. Puffed up in triumph, Monsieur Kamel watched him go with a threatening gaze, the finger pointing in Riad's direction shaking perceptibly. The boys at the back of the classroom were quiet. No one was brave enough to reveal the guilty party. Riad opened the door. Suddenly, we heard a loud noise. The sound of footfalls echoed in the halls and the stairwells, like a pack of hyenas in pursuit of their prey. I got up from my seat and looked outside. A crowd was making its way toward our *lycée*. In the schoolyard, some students had climbed onto others' shoulders; some were throwing rocks. We caught the lyrics from patriotic songs.

"What's going on?" asked Monsieur Kamel. His voice was strained and his eyes had suddenly gone blank.

No one had time to answer. A rock smashed through the window. I managed to dodge the shards of glass by ducking. A second rock landed on Sonia's desk, and she broke into hysterical screams. Outside, the crowd was getting bigger by the minute and was heading straight for our building. Monsieur Kamel had mysteriously vanished. With far greater speed than I thought myself capable, I stuffed my notebooks into my schoolbag and attempted to thread my way through the crowd of fleeing students. My heart was pounding and fear surged over me. My nicely organized little world was collapsing like a tower of building blocks. "What could be happening?" I repeated over and over again.

TWO

Tunis, November 30, 2010

No DOUBT ABOUT IT, Mom was going to keep in touch, whether I answered or not. It was the fifth email she'd sent this morning. Was I okay, she wanted to know. Was I getting enough to eat, was everything calm in Tunis? Of course I was okay. And besides, what could possibly happen in this shithole of a country, where there were pick-up artists, robbers, and low-lifes everywhere you turn? Mom wanted me to learn Arabic, wanted me to learn about the monotonous life she'd had, wanted me to "get to know my Tunisian heritage" as she never grew tired of insisting, every day, back in Ottawa.

Hi Mom!

Everything is quiet. Right here, in front of the Bour-guiba Institute for Living Languages there are dozens of cops leaning against the wall. As if the whole thing would fall on their heads if they weren't holding it up. I can't tell whether it's to guard the synagogue a few yards down the street or to protect the foreign students coming in and out of the building where I go for my courses. Whatever the case, they flash us smiles and give compliments I can hardly under-stand. Yesterday I ate some douida *at Auntie Neila's. She stuffed me like I was a goose being fattened up. Was it ever delicious! Posters of the president are everywhere — he's got both hands over his heart and a smug smile on his face. You can't tell whether he's saying he loves his people or that he would love to crush them. Tunis is quiet. No revolution in sight. You're paying too much attention to those web sites. Here, nobody has heard a word about demonstra-tions, coal miners, deaths, or political prisoners. Do us both a favour: keep cool. Anyhow, I can't figure out this country of yours.*

Lots of love,
Lila

There, it was done. I'd answered her. Hopefully she'd stop sending me those hysterical messages. I couldn't wait to get back to Ottawa. Tunis was not my hometown, even though Mom never stopped talking about her birthplace—the narrow streets, the old city, the *medina*, the warmth of the people, the blue sky, and easy living. I wasn't buying it. I was like a stranger here. Tunis was definitely not my home, even though I was staying with Mom's friends who were lovely people and treated me like their own daughter. No, Tunis was still a foreign city. I couldn't figure it out. I belonged in Ottawa where the trees in the parks changed colour with the seasons, where you have to run just to get across the wide streets, where there are museums that I practically grew up in and never get bored of because of the special exhibits. My hometown had dark, glacial nights when I could look up at the deep clear sky and feel my heart was at one with the boundless universe. The Ottawa River, with its broad banks and its convoluted meanderings, cut like a blade between two provinces. That was where I want to live, that was where I want to build my life. Not here, not in Tunis.

My phone vibrated. It was a text message from Mom. She was feeling reassured. Phew! I was just about to leave to visit my new friend, Donia. Actually, I was not quite sure she was my friend—let's call her my new classmate. I met her a couple of days ago in a cybercafé not far from Aunt Neila's. That's where I go to check my emails when there's no Internet connection at the house. Donia was the first to smile. The owner of the café was about to give me a hard time — you could tell by the grim look on his face. I couldn't stand the guy, it was true. There was something sneaky about him, the way he gave me the once-over. The day I met Donia, he wanted to charge me two dinars above the posted price. According to him, I'd been online fifteen minutes too long. You could tell from looking in his eyes that he was lying. His head was rolling from side to side like a fat watermelon on a flat countertop, and he was leering at my breasts. It was as if he was about to devour me. Swallow me. Luckily, Donia intervened.

"*Shnua*, Am Mokhtar!" she said, in a familiar, almost disrespectful, tone. "She's my guest, can't you see what a nice girl she is, just like me!"

She'd spoken glibly, like a little girl trying to butter up her father or grandfather. I just stood there, startled. I didn't know this girl with the sand-coloured skin, the radiant smile, and the black curly hair that fell to her shoulders. Why had she come to my defense? Why had she pretended I was her guest when I didn't even know her? And, as if by magic, it had worked. Donia's words seemed to have bewitched the café owner, Am Mokhtar. His gaze softened. He turned toward me with a resigned look on his face.

"I'm going to overlook it this time, because I respect Donia and because I'm really fond of her—she's like a daughter to me. You're her guest. So I'll forget the two dinars."

I felt like protesting, like showing that crook that I could do without his sudden politeness, but Donia didn't give me time to react. She guided me gently to the door, holding my arm as if we were old friends. I made no effort to stop her. *The "poor little Canadian" gets fooled again*, I thought. Outside, the wind was blowing as I'd never experienced it in this city. The clouds formed a thick grey blanket in the sky, one that would fall on our heads any minute. Fine grains of sand grated in my eyes.

"Donia's my name. Sorry about pretending to know you and all, but it was the only way I could rescue you from that guy Mokhtar. He knows he can't touch me. But I don't like him doing his shady dealings in front of me. I know them too well."

I stood there for a moment, startled, a blank look on my face. What could I say to this girl, who was about my age? Then, almost stuttering, I managed: "I'm Lila, and I'm here in Tunisia to improve my Arabic. I'm staying with friends who live down the street. Over there, see? The yellow building with the maroon windows."

I pointed to the building where Aunt Neila and Uncle Mounir lived. Donia, with her laughing eyes, shook her head. She seemed surprised to hear me speak with a slight accent.

"But what are you? Tunisian or foreigner?"

Even though I'm not entirely Tunisian, being called a "foreigner" ticked me off. I forced myself to smile and told her, "Well, I'm a little bit of both."

Donia noticed my reaction immediately. She put her hand to her mouth, by way of regret, then hurriedly added, "Really, I'm sorry. I didn't want to hurt your feelings, but I had no idea where you were from, I only wanted to help you."

And is if to make up for her comment about my background, she came closer to me. "You see that house across from us? That's where I live. If you want to use the Internet, come over. It's no problem."

Then she gave me her number and assured me I could call her whenever I felt like it.

Donia lived in a fine white house, with a white metal gate that protected a Mercedes 4x4 and a BMW sport model. A man wearing a burnouse was sitting in a plastic chair in front of the gate. He must be the watchman. The whole thing reeked of money. I slowly pulled out my phone to enter Donia's number. I didn't know what to do or what to think about this spontaneous girl who contradicted everything I'd learned about this city and its people.

"Thanks, Donia," I was finally able to articulate. "It's

really nice of you to help me out. I'll call you, that's a promise."

Was I really going to keep my promise? Not a morning went by that Aunt Neila didn't warn me about people who seem too eager to help. I believed every word she said. I'd been had more than once. There was something in my appearance, something about the way I looked at people, about my accent—something that told people that I was not really from here. So they tried to fool me, to raise the price, to convince me that their product was the best. Some even asked me to marry them! But Donia was different: she radiated kindness. My mother would say, "She's a nice girl." Well, well! I may have been far away, but here I was, using her expressions. What was happening? Was this city casting a spell over me?

Donia waved goodbye and turned away. Am Mokhtar came out in front of his shop and gave us a dirty look. When he saw me, he attempted to smile. He was missing two front teeth. Below his receding hairline, his forehead was furrowed with wrinkles. Funny, I almost felt sorry for him. But I quickly forgot his smile and made straight for Aunt Neila's building. A few drops of rain had begun to fall. The damp wind chilled my cheeks. This wasn't the kind of cold I was used to—it was nothing like the north wind that burns the tip of your nose in Ottawa. No, it was a damp, intense wind that penetrated right to the bone and chilled you from within.

This was another kind of nature. And it could be hard and unpredictable. Just like the people.

THREE

Tunis, January 3, 1984

I COULD BARELY FIND my way back to the classroom. The corridors of the *lycée* looked more like a railway station with passengers rushing every which way. I was shaking with fear but doing my best not to give in to panic. Everyone was pushing and shoving. From across the room I could see Sonia weeping and lamenting at the top of her voice. No one paid her the slightest attention. By now, the whole *lycée* was like a *souk* at peak shopping hour. Rocks were sailing in from all directions. I hid behind a pillar. I couldn't see hide nor hair of the principal, or the superintendent for that matter, the man we called Botti. All I could see were groups of shouting, frantic students rushing in all directions. *What should I do?* Heart pounding, legs quaking, I made for the fence to the west of the school. That was where Neila and I would clamber over the low wall when we were late for class—to avoid using the main entrance at the front of the building. We tried to make ourselves as tiny as possible to escape Botti's eagle eye, for he always lurked, ready for ambush, at that very spot, as though in a watchtower, the better to nab tardy students and would-be truants. Luckily for me, on that day Botti was nowhere in sight. The school authorities had vanished outright. Mustering what was left of my courage, I dashed down the corridor that passed behind the toilets. Usually, the foul stench would stick in your nose for several minutes. I didn't even notice this time. I could hear shouting. The students that had joined up with the terrifying hordes of hard-faced young men dressed in next-to-rags—who had emerged from God knows where to attack our *lycée*—were chanting political slogans: "Degree, no degree—no future!" Their words reverberated like the thud of a war drum. And all I wanted was to get my degree! What did these demonstrators really want?

I hid behind a bush. My whole body was shaking; I was holding my breath. But just as I was about to climb over the fence a powerful hand gripped me. Stopped in my tracks, I made no attempt to struggle. I thought it was the end of me; I could feel the sweat pouring down my back. Slowly I turned my head and, to my astonishment, saw Mounir. Neila's boyfriend, her lover. He lived up on the hillside that overlooked our neighbourhood in one of the slum dwellings built from pieces of sheet metal, stone, and dried mud. The families that lived there had left their native villages in the dry, dusty hinterland. They had a few sheep and goats, chickens and geese. The women tended the animals and the men sold charcoal from donkey carts. But ever since new housing projects had invaded the area — which used to be called *Kerch Al Ghaba*, "belly of the forest" — those same families had been forced out, moving from one temporary shack to another. Over time, the men began to sell manure, which was used in the gardens of the high-class villas that were popping up all around us like mushrooms. The women and girls would find work as maids or cleaning ladies in those same villas.

Mounir was the only member of his family to graduate from high school. He was tall, dark-skinned, with honey-coloured eyes, and he wore a perpetual sad smile on his face. Nights he worked as a security guard in the new shopping centre that catered to a well-to-do clientele from the more affluent areas. But he hadn't given up his studies; he attended university where he was studying law. His aim was to become a lawyer. Neila and Mounir had met at the shopping centre where she shopped for her family. Mounir was posted at the entrance to the supermarket where he inspected the bags of suspicious-looking customers. It had been love at first sight. "His eyes electrified me!" Neila told me later with a mischievous smile. From that moment on, they were always together. They would meet in secret, far from the terrifying gaze of Neila's father, Monsieur Abdelkader. It was an oasis of tenderness in the blazing desert of her father's rage. And I was the only one who knew their story — a simple, innocent love story that comforted me and amazed me, for in it I saw the power of love and how it could make people dream and inspire them with courage. Neila and Mounir's story, with their secret outings, the messages scribbled on pages torn from their school notebooks, and the strolls along the beach at La Goulette, reflected another reality, one that I knew only from the books I read and the films I saw with Neila. But there was nothing else in my life that spoke of love. Certainly not the marriage ceremonies my mother made me attend during the summer!

"Nadia, who's going to marry you if no one sees you at weddings?" And as though that wasn't enough to terrify me, mother went on, "You'll end up like your Aunt Rafika, that nasty old biddy."

So, against my will, fearing I would end up like my Aunt Rafika, I would put on my ruffled pink dress because it demurely displayed my narrow shoulders and my frail neck. Mother would always insist that I go to the hairdresser first. The "salon" occupied a rented garage at the end of our street.

"You're not going to attend my cousin's wedding with that frizzy hair of yours, are you? It looks like a horse brush. What will the guests think? That I can't even afford a two-dinar permanent for you?"

My mother always won. I never had the strength to resist her snide remarks and her devouring will. After being subjected to the burning hot air of the dryer and the curlers that pricked my scalp like hedgehog spikes, my hair came out straight and smooth, and fell down my back. So, dressed in my ridiculous pink gown, which had shrunk from repeated washing and drying and ironing, my hair straightened and fluffed up by the summer evening humidity, I tagged along with my mother to those fabulous weddings. The newlyweds would never kiss. "It's *ib*, you don't do it in front of others," my mother would hiss by way of disapproval at the kisses we'd occasionally see on TV. As if to confirm her judgment, my father would abruptly shut off the set and send me to my room to finish my homework even when I didn't have any homework or I'd done it all. The weddings I attended seemed dull, monotonous. The bride sat there in a gilded armchair, a bad copy of a Louis XVI fauteuil. A clothesline with red, green, and blue light bulbs stretched above her head. She held a lavish bouquet of jasmine and rarely smiled. Was she afraid of the new life that awaited her? The groom, too, stayed seated for the entire ceremony. He always wore a black suit and his hair was always combed carefully to one side. His bouquet was much smaller than the bride's, and he would constantly bring it up to his nose, either to breathe in its perfume or conceal his anxiety. The music was deafening. The band, which generally performed for a pittance, played all the popular songs I'd heard on the radio ever since I was five or six years old. The only part of the whole ceremony that really interested me was the moment when they served the crunchy almond baklava with fresh-squeezed lemonade, strawberry juice, or *gazuz*. The newlyweds never danced, never held hands. I never saw the slightest sign of love or affection. Nothing at all like the long, loving looks Neila traded with Mounir. Their wedding would be different. I was sure of it.

But there, perched on the wall that encircled our *lycée*, one arm around my school bag, and the other in Mounir's powerful grasp, weddings were the last thing on my mind.

"You shouldn't have come to school today. Hurry, get home as fast as you can," he told me.

His eyes were bloodshot, his hair tousled. I'd never seen him that way before. If I hadn't known him, I would just as well have taken him for a peasant, or for a member of the gang of young men I'd just avoided in the schoolyard. I couldn't utter a word. I sat there mute, paralyzed with fear. Mounir released my arm, and I nearly fell to the ground, but he held me by a shirttail. Finally I answered him, "I had no idea this was going to happen, no one told me there would be demonstrations."

Mounir's face grew darker still.

"Come on, let me help you climb over the wall," he said, as if to hide his concern. With one rapid movement he jumped to the ground, then held his hands together to make an impromptu step. "Put your left foot here, and don't be frightened, I'm strong enough to hold you."

I obeyed Mounir without a second thought. I was in shock; I had no idea what he was doing there, or why he was in such a state.

"Listen carefully, Nadia. There are huge demonstrations all over the city. The poor are rising up against the rich, against the people who have it all. We've come out into the streets for justice, and for bread. The police are everywhere — they're shooting people. Be careful, and go home as fast as you can. And don't tell anyone you saw me."

He hesitated.

"If you see Neila, say hello for me. Most of all, give her a kiss for me."

I blushed. "*Ib!*" mother would have said. But Mounir's words calmed me instead of making me tense.

"For sure. I promise!"

There was no time for another question. Mounir had already vanished behind the bushy eucalyptus that lined the other side of the wall. Lost like an ant in the dark foliage, swept up by a whirlwind. I had no idea what was going on. Revolt; the rich; the dispossessed. Who was against whom? Was I rich in Mounir's eyes? And if I was, why had he helped me? And what was his role — what did he have to do with all this? What group did he belong to? "We've come out into the streets for justice and for bread," is what he told me. Who exactly was "we"? My eyes began to blur. I felt a lump in my throat blocking my vocal chords. My clean and meticulously ordered world was collapsing, one organ at a time. In rapid succession. So, there were things I should have known but didn't. A loud crack made me jump. Gunfire. I set out as fast as my legs would carry me, faster than during physical education class at the *lycée*. My brain had sent out a distress call, and my feet, my legs, and my arms were responding.

FOUR

Tunis, December 4, 2010

WHAT A GORGEOUS CAFÉ with a view out over the Tunis lagoon! I could hardly believe I was in the same town. I couldn't stop looking at the lake. The dwarf palms planted randomly on the lawn made the view even more striking. Inside, the atmosphere was warm and enveloping, the people civilized, the drinks exquisite. Boys and girls were sitting together, side by side. Most were speaking French with the odd expression in Tunisian Arabic thrown in. I couldn't hear a single discordant voice. For the first time since I'd arrived, I felt calm, relaxed, and far away from the suffocating feel of the streets of Tunis that I passed through every day on my way to my Arabic courses or to go shopping with Aunt Neila at the market. The day after the incident with Am Mokhtar I called Donia to thank her. Before she hung up, she insisted I go with her to the Mezza Luna.

"It's a café for young people, I go there with some friends. We spend the afternoon, and later we go bowling. You'll get to know them. You'll like them — they're cool, just like you!"

I wasn't entirely certain that I wanted to go with Donia or get to know her friends. What did I possibly have to say to them? Why would I possibly like them, what could I possibly have in common with them? Sure, my mom was Tunisian, but my dad was Canadian. I'd lived my whole life in Canada. Most of my friends were Canadian. I spoke Arabic with an accent. In spite of my mom's attempts to give me a Tunisian identity, I really couldn't identify with the Tunisians around me.

And yet, sitting in the roomy café, I felt almost at home. The peals of laughter, the sound of coffee cups clinking against their saucers, the tinkle of ice cubes, the hiss of mint tea being poured, foaming, into handsome small tumblers decorated with arabesques. I slouched back in my armchair, at ease, feeling almost relieved, and looked around me. Donia was seated to my left. She was the leader of the group; that much was clear. Politely but firmly she held the attention of the young men who looked up to her as though she was one of them. Two boys and two girls made up the group. One of the boys, Jamel, was closest to Donia. Slender, seething with energy, words came out of his mouth easily. His glasses made him look like an intellectual; he appeared to be the smartest of the lot, the one to watch. Was he Donia's boyfriend? Could they be lovers? I suspected it, but there was nothing to confirm it except for the odd glance that lasted a little bit longer than it should, or a word that brought a smile to both of their faces. Call it a barely concealed sign of complicity, the kind of body language only the two of them could decipher. The other boy, Sami, had a shy, reserved look about him. His fine hair framed his face, giving him the appearance of a well-behaved young girl. He smiled frequently at Donia and continually nodded his head to agree with everything she said, but he spoke very little. The two girls were called Reem and Farah. They giggled to themselves as they glanced at one another, flickering their eyelids. One had her hair done pageboy style, slicked down, and a button nose, light-coloured skin, and slightly slanted eyes that made her look like a cat about to pounce. The other was constantly adjusting her abundant chestnut hair with the back of her hand. Her black eyes accentuated the whiteness of her skin; a few reddish blotches marked her oval face. Reem and Farah looked me over carefully when they saw me come in with Donia. Even before we were introduced, I knew they wouldn't like me. My ripped jeans, my multiple earrings worn in a line along my earlobe, the high forehead I'd inherited from my mom, and my blues eyes, just like my dad's: everything about me told them just how foreign I was. Even my brown and hope- lessly curly hair that stood out in corkscrew-like tufts from my head—another hand-me-down from Mom and a source of wonder, of compliments, and admira- tion during my childhood in Canada—was not enough for them to see me as a Tunisian. Me, the daughter born of the marriage of Nadia the Tunisian and Alex the Can- adian. In their eyes, I was some kind of strange mix, a hybrid, a monstrosity produced by the meeting of two distinct worlds but clearly belonging to neither. For the time being I tried to forget the wrenching adolescent metaphysical dilemmas that kept me awake at night; it was enough to bathe in the warm and welcoming atmosphere of the café. Next to me, Jamel was speak- ing in a low voice.

"Listen, you guys, it looks like things are getting out of hand online. I heard from a friend that a girl we know who writes a blog was arrested two days ago."

Donia's face went livid. I couldn't tell which it was: the shock of the news or anger. Reem and Farah exchanged whispers as they glanced sidelong at two tall young men who had just walked into the café. The news caught Sami's attention. His expression turned serious, his eyebrows raised; he wanted to ask a question. He opened his mouth, but remained silent. Words betrayed him. Only his glance followed. Donia asked Jamel in a low voice:

"This blogger, do you know who she is? Who told you the news? Don't tell me its Tounsia two-twelve."

Suddenly things turned serious. Jamel hesitated, then threw a quick glance in my direction. Donia appeared to understand his questioning look.

"Speak up already! We're all friends here," she ordered him, with emphasis on the "all" as she looked at me.

I sat there, motionless, barely understanding what they were talking about, but making an effort to get nearer to them, to take an interest in the discussion. Donia sensed I was ill at ease.

"Here, political dissidents are arrested and thrown in jail. It's forbidden to talk about politics, there's no freedom of speech. You draw a caricature of someone, and you take a big risk," she explained, never taking her eyes off Jamel.

Her voice was wavering and she spoke softly so as not to attract attention. But no one was watching us; there was laughter all around. People had come to the café to have a good time, not to talk politics. Reem and Farah got up to go to the washroom, leaving Jamel and Sami around our table. I dared to ask, "What are they writing, these cyber-dissidents? What are they upset about?"

Jamel leaned over and whispered in my ear: "Poverty, sky-high prices, injustice, dictatorship and nepotism, no work for the young. The blogger they just arrested, she's one of them."

Jamel's outburst startled me. I'd never given Tunisian politics a second thought. Why should I? True, I agreed to come here to improve my Arabic and to get to know Tunisian culture, but that was it. "Maybe a trip to Tunisia will help you get to know yourself better," was how Mom put it. The way she described her country, it was heaven on earth, a place where living was easy, and where relationships were warm and vibrant. A place where everything was sunbeams and sweetness. Deep inside, I knew Mom was laying it on thick in an attempt to persuade me. I knew she was looking at her homeland through a romantic lens, not to mention a strong dose of nostalgia; she'd been away for so long. But if she were ever to come back, she wouldn't know which way to turn. Still, I wanted to seize the opportunity — to believe Mom's words and try to find answers to my questions about my roots, my life, my future. After weeks of saying no, after weeks of indecision, I made up my mind. I put off my university registration for a semester, packed my bags, and arrived in Tunis to stay with Mom's best friends, Auntie Neila and Uncle Mounir.

What did I know about Tunisian politics, about

dictatorship, injustice, oppression, or cyber-dissidents? Mom may have mentioned them, but I hadn't been paying attention. She was always talking. Even the last few days, when she called or sent four or five text messages a day, I didn't take her seriously. She was getting worked up for nothing. But what if she was right? What if something weird was going on in this country that looked as if it were fast asleep? Could Donia, her pals, and my mom be right?

Donia was jiggling her leg; she looked really worried. Jamel put his hand on her shoulder and said in a low voice, "Do me a favour and stop moving your leg like that, you're making me nervous."

Without looking at him she stopped. Sami smiled timidly; you could feel the tension growing. "Do you think this is it? That things will really change?" he finally blurted out.

Jamel and Donia looked at him. I watched in silence. Reem and Farah came back from the washroom, their hair nicely arranged and their makeup refreshed. Clearly they weren't living on the same planet.

Donia was the first to respond: "I don't have the remotest idea! If it turns out they've arrested Tounsia two-twelve, that means they're panicking, going after the small fry. Everybody knows that what Tounsia two-twelve says on her blog is, it's almost..." She paused for a moment as she searched for the missing word. Like magnets attracted by the opposite pole, we drew close to her, to hear her. Her voice was faint, barely audible. "Almost banal, that's what I meant to say. Yes, that's it—banal."

Jamel took up where she'd left off: "But that's what the regime hates most of all. They want everybody to believe that everything is for the best in the best of all possible worlds."

Sami smiled and blinked. "Yes, that's it, a world of hypocrites."

His comment, sharp and to the point, made us all smile at once. But it also broke the ice, and the tension that had been building for the last few minutes melted away. Donia peeked at her phone.

Then she slowly turned her head toward Jamel, pointing a threatening finger at him. "Hey you! Watch yourself. Call me whenever you like, but no funny stuff."

Jamel said nothing, but his face was relaxed. He threw her a knowing glance. Sami got to his feet.

"Guys, I've got to go, my father made a scene the last time I got in late."

It was all Reem and Farah could do to stifle a sly smile as they chattered in low voices while looking at Sami. We all stood up. Donia paid for her mint tea and for mine as well. I didn't even have time to object. Sami had already left. Reem and Farah spotted another group of young people they seemed to recognize and excused themselves and went off to join them. Donia pretended not to have noticed the whole thing. Outside, the sun was about to set. I noticed a European-looking gentleman jogging along the embankment overlooking the lake. It was as if I were back in Ottawa, near the Byward Market. The cafés, the restaurants, the people going by on bikes, the outdoor shows. A vision flashed through my mind and then vanished like the sun whose last rays I saw reflected on the buildings and cars. Jamel was speaking to Donia in a low voice. I couldn't understand everything, but I picked up the words "demonstration" and "revolt."

Donia came over to me and exclaimed, "What a beautiful view! If you don't mind, it's time to go home. We can go bowling some other time."

I nodded without paying her too much attention. I was thinking about Jamel and Donia's words. I wanted to know more. Donia drove her own car. Everyone was silent on the trip home. Jamel was sitting in the back seat; I sat in the passenger seat. Tunis was preparing for night. The streetlamps were coming on and the white glare illuminated the gathering dusk. Battered old yellow buses were carrying people back home from work. Donia dropped Jamel off at a station. He waved to us before disappearing into the crowd. *Le passage*, read the sign above the station entrance.

"Does he live far from here?"

"He lives in Ettadamoun Township. He gets there by light rail," Donia answered.

"That's a funny name! Doesn't it mean 'solidarity'? I think I came across the word in my Arabic class. Why should there be a township called 'solidarity'?"

"I don't know. It's a populous area, pretty poor actually. Maybe we need more solidarity with those people." Then she added, "So, did you like my friends?" asking with her usual frankness, which I was coming to appreciate more and more.

"Yes! The whole evening was surprising and exciting. I learned a lot about Tunisia, about politics. It was nothing like my Arabic courses, where you die of boredom," I answered, letting down my guard for the first time since I got to Tunisia.

Donia's face lit up; she liked what I said.

"Well, I don't think you'll be disappointed. I'm sure there'll be more in the next few days."

She was referring to things I knew nothing about. I didn't want to put her on the spot, so I pretended not to understand exactly what she meant. She turned on the radio and a song in Arabic came on. I'd never heard the rhythms before. "It's my favourite," she said with a wink and a grin. Surprised, I found myself moving to the beat and humming the chorus. Clearly, Donia had more surprises for me. When her car stopped in front of Aunt Neila's place, the song had ended. Donia put her arms around me and gave me a gentle hug.

"My heart is never wrong. Something tells me we're going to be good friends, I know it."

I didn't reply, but I did return her hug. Then she got back into her car and drove off. The sound of the motor disappeared in the night. I pushed open the heavy door to the building. *OUT OF ERDOR* was written in large, jagged letters on a piece of brown cardboard stuck to the elevator door. I smiled at the misspelling. But I wasn't looking forward to climbing eight flights of stairs. With a grimace, I put my foot on the first step.

FIVE

WHEN I FINALLY REACHED home, I was gasping for breath. My lungs felt as if they were about to burst. Air, I needed air. I felt like sitting down to get some relief. My legs were shaking like reeds in the wind. One more step and I would flop down on the ground like a corpse, never able to get up again. I'd taken the same path home from the *lycée* hundreds of times before with Neila, carefree, chatting about our courses, making fun of our instructors' curious behaviour. But on that day, the same path seemed to have been the longest of my life. A passage of death. Down deserted streets I'd rushed. No bus, not one car or honking horn, no one strolling nonchalantly along the sidewalks. Shutters were closed tight. Carpets, which had been hung out on windowsills in the morning to air, had been brought in ahead of time. The freshly washed sheets and clothing that would normally be fluttering in the wind on rooftops or balconies had disappeared, pulled in by unseen hands. Farther off, at the base of the hills that rose up beyond our house, I could see black smoke rising into the sky, as if someone were cooking over an immense campfire. What had happened in these last few hours? I shoved open the wrought iron gate that led to our front door. Mother opened the door and pulled me inside, slamming it behind me. I faltered, almost fell to the floor, but she held me upright. There I stood, looking like an idiot.

"What's going on?" I asked Mother, in a faint voice.

Mother's round, pudgy face comforted me. Her sweet and harmonious features had the effect of calming syrup sliding into my mouth and soothing my parched throat. Slowly, I came back to my senses. My chest had stopped heaving; once again I was breathing normally.

"Bread riots! The people want bread!" Father called out from the living room, his ear glued to the radio.

"Bread riots? Where, when? There was a big demonstration at our *lycée*. Is that why the police were firing in the air?"

As she heard my words, mother's composure collapsed. She grimaced, face ashen.

"I hope no one was hurt or killed," she said, through pursed lips.

I shook my head.

"But I saw smoke rising, burning tires maybe. I don't have the faintest idea."

As she attempted to explain what was happening, Mother got ahold of herself. She handed me a glass of water.

"Najwa's mother Hedia told me this morning that the poor people in the El Omran, Ibn Khaldun, and Ettadamoun Townships can't afford bread, couscous, and pasta anymore. With the latest increases, the price of a baguette has doubled, people are going hungry. What an unjust policy! What a stupid government!"

I sat down at the kitchen table, an antiquated affair with wobbly legs that papa had never taken the trouble to fix. It was covered with checked oilcloth. Mother had closed the kitchen shutters. The light was fading, as was my heart. Deep down I knew it: my life wouldn't be the same. I gulped down a couple of mouthfuls of water. Now the pieces of the puzzle were beginning to fit together. I would never have believed that people would come out into the streets to express their anger. I'd only read about demonstrations in books. The previous summer I'd read Émile Zola's *Germinal*. The miners' strength of character captivated me, and I'd thought long and hard about the character of Étienne Lantier, the hero of the story, the leader of the strike, and his dreams of justice and equality. Things like that happened only in France, I thought.

Nobody talked about such conflicts in Tunisia — or not in our house, at least. On television we heard the directives of President Bourguiba, the Father of the Nation, the supreme combatant. If I happened to turn on the television when one of his directives was being broadcast, my first reaction was to switch it off. If I had nothing better to do, I would stay tuned, but I could never understand what he was talking about. It was a mishmash of historical anecdotes, of laughter and tears, of sniffling and moralizing. Everyone loathed the regime, but everyone pretended to like it in order to survive, to feed their children, and to be like everyone else. Father was like everybody else. He said nothing, listened to the news on the radio, watched television, muttered insults directed at God knows who, and life went on. At the *lycée* there were three groups: the children of the rich, of the poor, and of all the rest.

Neila and I belonged to the third group. We weren't rich, but we weren't poor either. The children of the rich came right up to the main entrance in chauffeur-driven cars. They wore name-brand clothing and enjoyed winter sports in the French or Swiss Alps. In summer they took up residence in Hammamet, on Cap Bon, where most of their families owned villas.

We could barely see the poor. It was as if they wanted to hide, as if their very presence was an irritant. It was hard to tell whether we couldn't see them or they made themselves invisible, for fear of humiliation. They were from the shantytowns, the same places where Mounir and his family lived. Not too long before, Mother had mentioned that the government planned to demolish the shantytowns and build social housing, with running water, sewers, and electricity. Perhaps it was a way to make poverty easier to swallow. But I didn't know whether the project had ever come through. Neila would have known; she would have told me.

Then there were the people like Neila and me. Our parents were civil servants. We lived alongside the rich, but we weren't like them — by accident or happy coincidence. Father had always had difficulty making ends meet. Mother did not have a job, but she managed to balance the budget well enough to make our life comfortable, "like everyone else," as she would say. She did the cooking, darned the holes in Father's socks, and bought our clothing in second-hand shops.

"Don't you dare say where you get your clothes," she would repeat like a mantra, pulling down her lower right eyelid with her index finger to make sure I took her advice to heart. Whenever she bought me a skirt, a blouse, or a pair of trousers from the shops that sold second-hand clothing shipped from America, the watchword was always the same.

"What if somebody asks me where I bought them?" I replied naively.

Mother lost her temper. She didn't like my stupid questions. She would throw me a dark glance that made my blood run cold.

"Tell them your uncle brought them from France!"

My lesson learned, I didn't say another word.

One day, Neila asked me where I'd bought the pleated red-and-blue plaid skirt I was wearing.

"My uncle brought it for me from France," I answered, lowering my eyes to avoid her gaze.

"Oh, me too! My uncle brought me this big brown sweater from France!"

Without saying as much, we each understood that we were obeying orders from our mothers, and that in reality we belonged to the "others" — that group of people neither rich nor poor. The ones caught between the two extremes, like hostages. We were part of that famous middle class that was getting poorer and poorer by the day, but that still insisted on balancing its budget, on saving face, and on living like everybody else.

Father came into the kitchen. For the first time, I noticed how frail and fragile he had become. His thinning hair was plastered to his skull like a spider web. The wrinkles on his forehead had gotten deeper with age. His slightly slumped back seemed even more hunched than usual. I didn't know whether it was due to the day's events, or whether the shock I'd experienced had opened my eyes and made me see the world in a different light.

"Nadia, why are you so upset?" he asked me. "It's nothing. It'll all be over soon, you'll see."

He was lying and I knew it. He wanted to reassure me. Mother was pretending not to hear a thing; she was boiling water to cook macaroni for the evening meal.

Suddenly we heard a loud boom, an explosion very close to our house. Mother clapped her hand to her heart and lifted her eyes skyward.

"Oh my God! Whatever is happening?"

Shots rang out. Father went to open the kitchen door that led to the garden to find out what was going on. He was determined to calm us down.

"It's nothing, it's nothing," he repeated. "Must be rubber bullets."

Mother's look was anything but happy.

"Don't open that door, do you want to kill us all or what?"

Father backed up, hurried out of the kitchen, and went back into the living room. I could hear the sound of the radio, but the words were cold and incomprehensible.

"There's a curfew in effect, no one can go outside

after eight o'clock," he informed us mechanically from the living room.

I thought of Neila. How was she experiencing these moments? And Mounir, what was he doing right now? Was he one of the demonstrators, those "gangs of hooligans," as everyone called them? Suddenly I was worried about him; I could understand his anger, the frustration that radiated from him, and the injustice in society that he was determined to fight. I visualized him as Étienne Lantier, exhorting his friends to revolt, resisting with clear eyes, against the foremen, against the oppression of the nouveaux riches who shamelessly displayed their ill-gotten wealth and stole the livelihood of the poor. I missed my two friends. I would have liked to be with them, to talk about what was happening, to get a grasp on things, to find out who was on the side of good, who was on the side of evil. Which way was up, which way was down?

I went to my room. Our little neighbour Najwa was there. She would come over from time to time to spend the day at our place or take a nap in my room. It was her reward for good behaviour. She was six years old and just starting school. So there she was, playing with her doll and sniffing constantly as she did. No sooner did she see me than she threw herself into my arms.

"Oh Nadia, there you are! Come play with me, please!"

She squinted and brought her finger to her temple in a childish gesture intended to charm me. I smiled. Then I kissed her and promised I'd play dolls with her when I was a little more relaxed. My head was spinning like a weathercock in gale-force winds. Would school be open tomorrow? Too bad papa never had a telephone installed. How I would have liked to talk to Neila! I couldn't even slip outside and hurry down the street to Hassan's, the neighbourhood grocer. At least he had a telephone. And if I slipped him a one hundred-millime coin he would let me call my friend.

Without a telephone, I consoled myself by imagining that Neila was safe.

Later, we were all sitting in the living room, each of us balancing a plate of macaroni on our laps. It was still early in the month, meaning that everyone was entitled to a meatball. Normally we would take our meals around the kitchen table. But that day, every-thing was special. At first, Mother had refused to let us eat in the living room, but she finally relented. So we filled our plates with macaroni and sat down in front of the old black-and-white television set. Najwa was there with us. She couldn't really understand what was going on, but she was happy that we were together. She was careful not to let any crumbs fall on the tile floor. If she did, Mother would scold her: "Be careful, sweetie, or I won't let you come visiting anymore." But that evening no one was paying attention to the macaroni that slithered off our plates or the tomato sauce that stained the arms of the threadbare armchairs in our blue living room.

Our eyes were glued to the tiny screen. What we saw stunned us: burned-out cars, overturned buses. The police were firing; people were fleeing. Stones were being thrown in all directions, shop windows shattered. Smoke obscured the view, like an early morning mist. Soldiers had come out of their barracks, tanks lined the main streets of the capital. I could no longer recognize Avenue Bourguiba; it had become a battlefield, or a set from some war movie. There I was, sitting in front of the TV set, eyes focused on the pictures. Who were these people who'd come out into the streets and were defying the police and the army? How many of them were there? As I watched the images, I realized for the first time in my life that the cocoon in which I'd been living for the last eighteen years was nothing but a flimsy partition that kept me from seeing the other reality, that of the poor and the downtrodden, of those who suffer in silence.

Father's silence had nothing to do with theirs. He kept his powerlessness to himself. He was afraid of contaminating us with his ideas, afraid of sharing his bitterness, his cowardice. He feared Mother, her sharp tongue. On that day, too, I understood Mother's

hypocrisy. She knew we weren't rich, but she was determined to keep up appearances at all costs, to make it
seem as though we were just like everybody else. But
who was this "everybody else"? Weren't they all just
like us?

That night, after I'd helped Najwa brush her doll's
blond nylon hair and dress it in a too-tight skirt and a
piece of fabric sewn into a tube to hide the breasts, I
slipped quietly into my bed. The flickering blue flame of
the kerosene heater reflected against the ceiling. In the
darkness, I imagined fleeting forms dancing and shifting like shadow puppets. Najwa was breathing heavily.
Her stuffed nose snorted like a tractor struggling to
extricate itself from the mud. I made myself a promise:
tomorrow, I would begin my search for the truth. No
longer would it be enough to be a good student, obey
my parents and my instructors, or buy a telephone with
my first paycheck. Life was much more complicated.
Now I was certain of that.

S I X

Tunis, December 4, 2010

Aunt Neila and Uncle Mounir made an odd couple. Light years away from Mom and Dad's noisy relationship. There was sadness in Aunt Neila's eyes that never left her, even when she smiled. It was as though she and sadness were one and the same. More than a few times since I'd been staying with them, I'd come upon her crouched on her prayer mat, bent forward, thighs touching her stomach, head hung low as if she was a prisoner of war. The only difference was the way she held her hands in front of her, almost completely covering her face. When she would get up from the prayer, I didn't dare look her in the eye. I felt like vanishing, or making myself invisible so as not to disturb her.

"How was your Arabic class today?" she inquired in her high-pitched little girl's voice.

Her eyes were red. I pretended not to notice.

"Oh, not too bad," I would say, as I always do, in a nonchalant tone. "I don't know what good it's going to do me."

Then, with a rapid motion she removed her prayer cloak, showing her short black hair streaked with grey.

She would come over and kiss me on the cheek, just as Mom would do. The odour of rose water followed her, as inseparable from her as her shadow. I loved Aunt Neila dearly, but I didn't entirely understand why.

Uncle Mounir was another story altogether: something about him frightened me. Mostly it was his honey-coloured eyes. I could see hardness in them. Perhaps something had happened to him, something that changed his life. He always wore the same worn grey wool sweater. His curly hair was always carefully combed to the right. There was an old scar along his forearm, wide, swollen, like a snake glued to his skin. Its colour—darker than his skin—caught my eye. It was the first thing I noticed about him when he shook my hand. I noticed a faint smile on his lips when he saw me glance at the scar. A strange kind of smile that I couldn't place. Bitterness, pride, nostalgia, pain?

Aside from that slightly mysterious air, Uncle Mounir seemed normal enough. He never raised his voice. Only rarely could I hear him from my room: "Neila," he would call out, "would you make me a coffee please?" Almost imploring. Soon after, the strong smell of coffee came wafting from the kitchen, floating across the living room to my room, tickling my nostrils. I was no coffee drinker, but each time I smelled it, the odour dazzled me like the first rays of spring sunshine. I breathed it in deeply, filling my lungs. Coffee was the only thing Uncle Mounir asked his wife to prepare for him. Often I would see him cooking, a *fouta* wrapped around his hips and his old sweater over his shoulders and chest. He fried the sliced potatoes in boiling oil and the smoke rose up like a volcano erupting after a long slumber. Today, he was fixing *keftaji*.

"It's poor people's food," he announced, to make me laugh.

Aunt Neila smiled. The wrinkles around her eyes formed half-moons that intersected as if to keep each other company. But there was always sadness in her gaze, always the same melancholy. She opened her mouth to say something, but thought better of it. Still that same look in her eyes.

"Is it really true, Aunt Neila? Do poor people really eat *keftaji*?"

"Sort of. It's street food. Everybody likes it, young and old, rich and poor. It's like hotdogs there where you live, in America," she answered.

Uncle Mounir was dropping vegetable slices into the bubbling oil. First came the red and green peppers, followed by chunks of squash. Uncle Mounir knew what he was doing. His movements were skilled and rapid. *Keftaji* was a culinary delicacy. Once fried, the vegetables were finely chopped, mixed, and spiced. A fried egg nestled in the centre of each plate, like the sun in the middle of the sky. Mom never cooked this dish for me. It was one of the best I've tasted since I arrived in Tunisia.

Every night after the late news, Uncle Mounir took a seat on the balcony and smoked a cigarette. I knew he was finished when the yellow light of the bare bulb hanging from the ceiling of the balcony switched off and no light shone into my bedroom.

When Aunt Neila and Uncle Mounir talked, it was mostly a monologue: the words went one way, from uncle to aunt. She listened with a certain detachment, as if her mind were wandering, but her eyes were full of love. She never contradicted him; she was there for him, like the pillar that supports the dome. But she was a fragile pillar, one with invisible cracks. Mom always has something to say; there was always something in her voice when she talked with Dad. Not Aunt Neila. Not in front of me in any event.

When I came back to the apartment out of breath from climbing eight flights of stairs, I could only think about one thing: getting some sleep. The meeting with

Donia and her friends and the discussion about the social situation in Tunisia had worn me out. I needed calm in order to get a grip on things.

Aunt Neila and Uncle Mounir were sitting in front of their TV. The apartment was almost completely dark; a floor lamp was on in a corner. Light from the screen illuminated the room. It was like a movie theatre, with lights bright, then dim. My arrival disturbed the calm atmosphere.

"So, how was it, your meeting with your friends?" Uncle Mounir asked, with a knowing grin.

"I hope you got along with Donia and her pals," added Aunt Neila.

I sat down close to them in a grey armchair. My knee joint was creaking. My muscles were stiff and were not responding to my brain. The climb up the stairs had exhausted me. I put my hand on my knee and gave myself a quick massage.

"Yes, I had a nice afternoon with Donia and her friends. The view over the lagoon was magnificent."

I didn't say a word about the blogger who had been arrested, or about the political discussion I'd heard. I pretended everything was normal. Aunt Neila seemed relieved by my answer, but Uncle Mounir wanted to know more.

"These friends of hers, they pulled up in BMWs of course, good-looking guys, from good families."

Now he wasn't speaking in Arabic, but in French with a strong accent, rolling his *r*'s. There was a touch of sarcasm in his words, but I couldn't figure out what he was leading up to.

"Well, Donia drives a car. I don't remember what kind it is. But I'm not sure the others have one. She drove one of them to a metro station. He was on his way to Etta . . . Ettadamoun Township, I think that's what it was."

The name had a strange effect on Uncle Mounir. His gaze softened. Aunt Neila smiled, and came to my rescue: "Uh, it's a poor part of town."

Uncle Mounir scratched his scar. There was a hint of wistfulness in his eyes; he dropped his resentful attitude. "Ettadamoun Township, that's where real men come from."

Then he got to his feet and went into the kitchen. Something in his movements gave me the idea that he wanted to say something, but an obstacle, a solid, impenetrable wall impeded him.

I looked at Aunt Neila, confused and inquisitive at the same time.

"How come Uncle Mounir doesn't seem to like rich people? Why does he seem to like the poor without even knowing them?"

Aunt Neila came over to me. I saw the same sadness that always seemed to lie deep in her eyes. She put her hand on my shoulder. I caught the scent of rose water. I smiled at her.

"It's a long story. Didn't your mother ever tell you? I thought you knew everything about us."

I shook my head. Mom had always spoken of her friends with admiration, with enchantment. She wanted me to spend my stay in Tunisia at their house. But she never said a word about their past. Suddenly Aunt Neila took my hand.

"You know something, Lila. If I had a daughter I'd like her to be like you—intelligent, forthright. But God did not grant me that gift. Perhaps He will grant it to me in another life."

Her words threw me into turmoil. The hand that she grasped was shaking. Should I step away from her, or move even closer? Take her in my arms and kiss her? Tear away the veil of sadness that seemed to envelop her? I stood motionless, unable to speak.

Uncle Mounir came from the kitchen with a platter full of oranges cut into quarters. Aunt Neila let go of my hand. A tear gleamed in the corner of her eye. She picked up a piece of orange and handed it to me. The scent of the fruit and its intense flavor reinvigorated me. Slowly, my strength returned. This city was setting a trap for me. I could feel it. Uncle Mounir and Aunt Neila were more than just mother's friends; they were part of a story and a past that was painful for some people, one that still captivated Mom. I was letting go of my indifference. Curiosity had penetrated my inner life; I couldn't hold back any longer. I was about to ask them how they met when Uncle Mounir put his finger to his lips.

The announcer on TV had just said the word "Tunisia." It wasn't a local station. Uncle Mounir was watching Al Jazeera, which was broadcasting from Qatar.

He turned to us and said in a serious voice: "People are going on strike in the south. Ben Ali can't be happy!"

I thought about the worried tone of Mom's messages. "So, Mom was right! Yesterday she was really nervous and upset. She was telling me that troubles were breaking out all over the country."

Aunt Neila nodded. "Yes, there are troubles, but you won't hear a word about them on local TV. Here, in Tunis, nobody knows anything. People are going about their business as if everything is fine."

So, my hosts knew exactly what was going on. Donia and her friends knew too. Even my mother, who was five thousand miles from here, knew. I was the only one, it seemed, who didn't know and hadn't wanted to know. I ventured: "The cyber-dissidents and the bloggers, the ones that are sent to jail because they criticize the dictatorship, have you heard about them?" I asked them, a worried look on my face, as though I'd just revealed a state secret.

Uncle Mounir and Aunt Neila seemed startled.

"How did you know? Where did you hear?" they asked in unison.

"From Donia and her friend Jamel, the one who comes from Ettadamoun. They brought it up."

Uncle Mounir and Aunt Neila stared at me, eyes full of wonderment, as if I were their baby and had just taken my first steps. Suddenly, I discovered two different people. A couple that was resisting in its fashion; a couple that had surrounded itself with silence to escape the past.

But what was the past that lay hidden behind their shadowed eyes, their sad smiles? That day, for the first time, I felt at ease in this land. I almost felt like staying longer.

SEVEN

THE BREAD RIOTS OR the couscous revolt: that's what they called it. That same revolt had opened my eyes, had shaken me out of my inertia, and forced me out of ignorance. Suddenly my little world had become too small. Revolt; it was the revolt that revealed the faces of the poor to me, the faces of the oppressed, of those who had been cast aside. The couscous revolt revealed Mounir's face to me. The real Mounir—not Mounir the model student who attended class during the day and worked at night as a security guard, not Mounir the prince charming Neila wanted to marry to escape her father's reign of terror, but Mounir the militant. The left-wing militant who did all his daily prayers. The half-Islamist, half-Communist militant. The militant who wolfed down the works of Karl Marx and Jean-Paul Sartre and Michel Foucault, who devoured the writings of al-Mawdudi and Sayed Qutb. The militant with the built-in, wall-to-wall contradictions. The revolt exposed that hidden face to me, when before it had been as obscure as the dark side of the moon. This was a side that neither my father nor Neila's were ready to acknowledge. The revolt had smashed the mask behind which Mounir had been hiding ever since we had known each other. The revolt brought us together, built a sense of solidarity that went beyond lighthearted jokes and small talk and established strong ties above and beyond the budding love between Neila and Mounir, and my affection for the two of them, my best friends.

The bread riots swept over me like a second adolescence. Like when I'd had my first period. When it hit, I panicked. Would my body bleed until I was emptied of my last drop? Mother looked at the white drawers I held out to her with a trembling hand. I was sure she would break into tears and rush me to the hospital to save my life. What a surprise: she burst out laughing!

"Now you're a woman," she told me. "Now you can have babies."

Then she handed me a piece of white fabric. A kind of small cotton napkin.

"Put this napkin in your drawers to keep the blood from staining. I've got plenty," she assured me with a smile on her lips. "Don't forget to rinse out the blood from the napkins, and don't let your father see them."

"But why am I bleeding? Do I have some sort of wound inside me?" I asked, more surprised than ever by mother's instructions.

"Every month your body gets ready to receive a baby — that's why there's all the extra blood. You'll be learning all about it in school. You'll see."

I did not answer, and I did exactly as mother told me. I asked her no further questions. The discussion was over. Within a few minutes, my sexual education had ended as quickly as it had begun.

That same day I shared the news with Neila.

"But what world are you living in? No one ever told you? That's all my aunts ever talk about."

"Well, you know I don't have an aunt, except for Auntie Rafika who does nothing but complain and is always depressed. She doesn't count," I fired back.

"Yes, I know," she said in exasperation, "but you could always open up a magazine, or read a book. Here," she said, pulling a magazine from under her mattress. "Take it and read it."

She handed me a magazine with a beautiful woman on the cover. Her blond hair tumbled down about her face. *Elle*, the magazine was called.

"Where did you find this?" I asked her, growing more startled by the moment.

"At Samia's, our neighbourhood hairdresser. Mother and I went to get our hair done. There's always a pile of magazines on the table in the middle of the salon. I just love the photos, and also the articles. Here's a whole feature on the monthlies."

"Monthlies," I repeated, shocked. "You mean our monthly exams?"

Neila suppressed another sigh of exasperation. "When are you going to grow up, Nadia? Monthlies, menstruation, the bleeding that comes every month. That's what I'm trying to tell you."

"Okay, okay, I was just kidding," I answered with a laugh and stuffed the magazine into my school bag.

At school, not one single natural science instructor ever mentioned monthlies, never breathed a word about reproduction. We dissected pigeons, frogs, and mice, but never mentioned humans.

So it was that I learned the facts of life thanks to Neila, to the magazines that we picked up at Samia the hairdresser's, or the famous *Larousse*, which Dalia, one of our classmates, would bring to school from time to time. It was a book on human reproduction, and it showed men and women nude. Dalia's mother was a physician. She had bought the book on a trip to France. That was how I taught myself, leafing through magazines and books and talking with Neila. But aside from these new insights, my life didn't change. I believed everything my parents told me, or sometimes didn't tell me. I attended school, did my homework, watched television, read books, and dreamed.

The bread riots had a powerful impact on me. Now I began to doubt everything: my classes, my parents, my country, my opinions about others, my reading, my instructors. The sight of overturned cars, the red flames rising from burning tires, the police shooting at demonstrators, the crowds surging through the streets, the frightened politicians making public declarations and announcements had awakened me from a long slumber, from the indolence I'd gradually sunk into along with everybody else.

But there was also the look in Mounir's eyes when he'd spoken to me before I clambered up onto the school wall. That look, where injustice mingled with oppression, and where fury struggled against madness. That look hasn't left me ever since. Now I understood that I could no longer live my life and overlook the suffering of others, could no longer think only of my family and myself. That look of his gave me the strength to reexamine my life, to criticize the choices my parents had made for me, and to make my own decisions.

I SPENT THE whole day at home. My parents didn't go out either. Najwa was still sniffling; all she wanted was for me to play with her. Again and again we dressed and undressed her doll. We combed its hair, but the tiny plastic brush got stuck instead of sliding smoothly through the artificial locks. And if we pulled too hard, the nylon strands popped out of the doll's head, to Najwa's dismay. She began to panic. All she could think of was her balding doll. So while she worried, I snuck out of the room and into the garden. It was winter. All the fruit trees—the apple, apricot, and peach trees—had lost their leaves. Only the disparate cypresses that lined the fence at the rear of our yard had kept their green. Their dry, brown needles covered the ground. I walked around the house in an attempt to steal a glance or two beyond the wall. Nothing. Not a single car. Only an occasional passerby, moving with rapid steps.

I climbed up into the enclosure that protected the gas and water meters. It was my personal observation post, the place from which I could see what was happening in the street without being seen. The corner grocer was closed. No bread delivery, no milk. The revolt was still going on. The bread riots. Further on, I spotted a black-and-white police van, the type we called *baga*.

It was parked. Two policemen were standing guard in front, smoking and talking. Their colleagues were crammed inside like sardines, shoulder to shoulder. I could see their gray-rimmed helmets through the windows. What could they be thinking about? About the young punks who, as recently as yesterday, were pelting them with rocks aimed at their heads? About their starvation wages, on which they could never hope to live like the masters they protected? Or about their families, their wives who were always asking for a bit more money, or about the price of bread and the high cost of living? The two cops kept smoking, sullen looks on their faces.

I noticed Hedia, Najwa's mother; her husband had recently died of a heart attack. She was crossing the street, dressed completely in black, a scarf covering her hair. Even at a distance, hurt seemed to glimmer in her eyes. She stopped in front of the grocery store. Did she want to buy some bread? Not a soul was there. Hedia paused for a moment, at a loss, hands crossed in front of her. Then she made her way back. There would be no bread for her children that day. She did not come to pick up Najwa. She knew her daughter was in good hands. And there would be one less mouth to feed.

I was just about to climb down from my observation post when I spotted Neila. She was heading for our house, long faced, clear eyed, hair pulled up into a ponytail. She passed directly in front of the *baga*. The two cops looked her over from head to toe as she walked by. Neila ignored them, walking with steady, rapid steps. She wanted to see me, I was sure of it. I made my way down from the enclosure and went over to open the garden gate. Neila stepped back, startled by my sudden appearance.

"How did you know I was here? I didn't even ring."

"I was watching you from my observation post," I said, pointing to my secret hideaway.

Neila brushed some strands of hair from her forehead. A veil of concern slipped across her face.

"Why didn't you come yesterday?" I asked. "I waited for you in front of your building as usual, but you never came down, and I had to go. Afterwards, you should have seen the *lycée*, Sonia yelling, the pushing and shoving in the corridors. And Mounir..."

"You saw him? Where? I saw the demonstrations on TV, but I haven't heard from him. He hasn't called me since yesterday morning." Her face darkened. She was hiding something from me.

"Come on in," I nearly ordered her.

Neila almost let herself be pulled inside. I let go of the wrought iron gate, which closed with a creak.

We went into my room and sat down. Najwa was in the kitchen, eating. I could hear her chatting with mother, who was cooking. Father was still in the living room, his ear glued to the radio, motionless; a block of stone that breathed. He was listening intently to one broadcast after another.

"How come you didn't come to school yesterday? On account of your father?"

Neila shook her head energetically. "I was coming down the stairs, on the way out of the building to meet you outside, as usual, there by the streetlight, when Mounir popped up from I have no idea where. He was waiting for me. He told me: 'Don't go to school today, Neila. There's going to be trouble. You know, the increase in bread prices has infuriated people across the country. Today that fury will reach Tunis and its suburbs. It won't be pretty to see. Better for you to stay at home.' His eyes weren't soft, like before. It wasn't the same Mounir. 'How do you know? How do you know that there are going to be demonstrations here, not far from our place?' I asked him, half-surprised and half-upset that he hadn't said a word to me the day before.

"You could see that Mounir was nervous. I could tell he wanted to be on his way as fast as he could. He was afraid that one of our neighbours might see him talking to me. He stood there, mouth closed, unable to say a single word. I looked him in the eye. I wanted to slap him, to shake him out of his silence. After a couple of minutes, he mumbled, 'I can't talk about it now, Neila. It's a long story. One day I'll tell you. Yes, I know things that you don't. Don't be disturbed if you don't hear from me in the next few days.' Then, as quickly as he appeared, he turned away and vanished. I don't have the faintest idea what he's doing or who he's working with. Nadia, I'm in a state of shock. All this time he's been lying to me. Me, who loves him and believes in him. Do you understand, Nadia? Mounir is a liar."

She was gasping now, barely able to speak; her eyes brimmed with tears. The deluge was about to break loose, but I managed to forestall it. Stepping close to her, I took her by the shoulders. Normally, Neila was the stronger of us. She was the one who kept me up to date on all the gossip at the *lycée*. One day she told me that Sonia had gone all the way. How we laughed that day!

"Gone all the way?" I'd responded, incredulous. "All the way to where? I'm surprised she tells you where she's going."

Neila laughed so hard that she just about peed. She crossed her legs and grasped her belly with both hands.

"What a dunce you are! Go all the way, that's when a boy and a girl have sex for the first time."

I blushed crimson. The blood was throbbing in my head. Even the mention of the subject had a powerful effect on me. At that instant, I was struck dumb.

Neila was still laughing at me, and I ended up bursting into laughter as well, to hide my ignorance and my embarrassment. Neila knew everything; I knew almost nothing. But today, as I held her in my arms, she felt weak, fragile, and about to collapse.

"It's okay, Neila. Calm down. Mounir is no liar. I saw him yesterday at school. He helped me climb over the wall to get away from the demonstrators who broke into our *lycée*. He's a militant, it's as simple as that!" I told her with fervour, my eyes gleaming like the eyes of a little girl blowing out the candles on her birthday cake.

Neila gently disengaged herself. She was no longer crying. Her face went back to normal. A faint smile fluttered on her lips.

"How do you know he's a militant? And for who, what?"

Her eyebrows knit as she awaited my response.

"I know it, I can tell in my heart. He's fighting for the poor. You'll see, he'll tell you. He wasn't lying to you — he was just hiding his other face. Did you watch the news last night?"

Neila nodded.

"Did you see the pictures of the young men throwing stones? Many of them were wearing hoods. Do you remember?"

A shadow passed over Neila's face.

"What are you getting at?"

I hesitated for an instant, then spoke. "I think Mounir was one of them, or he knows some of them."

"You've got to be joking!"

"It's no joke. I'm your friend. Look me in the eyes. Mounir is not a bum or a parasite, like they keep saying on the radio and the television. Mounir is a militant. Get it? Remember when we ran into him at the shopping centre, a year ago? He was carrying some books. Most of them were wrapped in newsprint. While you were talking with him I got a glimpse of the title of one of them through a tear in the paper. I'm certain it was *Capital* by Karl Marx."

Now it was Neila's turn to be shocked. She hadn't made the connections that I'd made only yesterday. Neila was still living in the stunted world of our parents. I had to rescue her. For the first time since we'd become friends, I felt more courageous than Neila, stronger, more motivated.

"Who is this Karl what's-his-name? And what does he have to do with what Mounir is doing? Eh? Enlighten me, if you please, smarty-pants." She'd adopted a sarcastic attitude because she couldn't believe that Mounir could act any differently than everyone else.

"Neila, listen to me. This isn't the time for snarky remarks. I know you're confused, and so am I. Karl Marx is the father of communism. I suspect that Mounir's involved in it. He's fighting for the rights of the poor, and against the injustice of the system—"

She wouldn't allow me to go on. "When did you read all that stuff? You're not going to tell me you're a militant too, and I'm the only one who doesn't know."

Her tears began to flow again. Like a gentle, persistent spring rain.

"Come on Neila, what are you talking about? I'm

not involved in anything. I'm just like you, trying to figure out which way to turn. I do read about communism, about socialism and other complicated subjects. I don't really understand that much, but at least I know the theory. What do you think I've been doing all summer?"

Neila was surprised. True enough, we'd spent most of the summer watching television together, going for long, aimless walks, picking jasmine blooms we'd make into garlands, or putting on the swimsuits we'd bought second-hand and sunbathing on the patio in my parents' garden.

"I read when my parents are taking their afternoon nap and I don't have anything else to keep me busy. My father keeps a lot of old books he buys from the second-hand book dealers in the Rue Zarkoun hidden in his closet. There was one on communism. I read it, and that's how I guessed that Mounir is one of those people."

She shook her head and looked away. Neila was still living in the past. From the kitchen, I could hear Najwa's sniffling like stuttering laughter. How badly I wanted Neila to listen to me!

EIGHT

Tunis, December 4, 2010

"LILA, ARE YOU SURE everything is okay there? Here, they're talking about it more and more on the news. It sounds serious, like the regime is on its last legs. Don't you want to come back to Ottawa?"

Mom's voice was coming through, without echo or interruption. Loud and clear, it lodged in my eardrum. But I couldn't understand why she was upset. Why was she so afraid, when she was the one who insisted I spend several months here? Funny, I didn't feel like I had to leave in a hurry. Leave now, when I was beginning to make friends and get to know Uncle Mounir and Aunt Neila? The idea seemed ridiculous. Only two weeks ago, I would have jumped for joy at the thought of packing my bags and flying home. Not anymore.

Today, I had to admit: something was keeping me here. An invisible magnet.

"I'm doing fine, Mom. Sure, there are some riots in the country, but that's in the small towns and villages. Here, in Tunis, everything's quiet, everything seems normal. Hold on a second—here's Aunt Neila. She wants to talk to you."

Aunt Neila came into the living room, still wearing her dressing gown. She smiled at me, and the sight of her face put me at ease. I gave her the handset and she winked at me by way of thanks. I sat on the sofa, resting my cheek in the palm of my hand. A bit discouraged, I listened to the conversation. Aunt Neila's face was shining. I had the impression that her habitual sadness had almost vanished. Mom's voice was magical; it worked miracles.

"Nadia, my dear Nadia, how are you? How happy I am to hear that beautiful voice of yours! How is Alex? And your job? Lila told me you're working for the Canadian government. *Mabrouk*, sweetie! I'm really proud of you!"

Aunt Neila fell silent for a brief moment. Her eyes were focused on some distant point. The window, the balcony, the far-off summit of Mount Boukornine, maybe even the horizon. She was listening to my mother intently, fiddling with the sash of her dressing gown at the same time. I imagined a young teenager, fragile but full of optimism, defying rigid structures and traditions. Another Aunt Neila, an aunt turned twenty years old at the sound of my mother's voice.

"Nadia, don't worry about Lila. She's our daughter, and you know it. No, there are no demonstrations in Tunis. Not so far, at any rate. Not as far as I know."

Then her youthfulness faded, as if a cloud had passed over her face. She became pensive. Her face turned forlorn, her eyes blank, her expression strained. Why? Her dainty mouth remained open. Her cheeks were drawn. She uttered a few incomprehensible words. Mother was still talking to her. Finally, she managed to answer.

"Mounir? How is he doing? You know. Nadia, he's not the same Mounir we knew back then. The old fire is gone. All those years in prison. I'm living in the shadow of the past."

I could feel my heart in my throat. I felt dizzy. Why was I sitting there, in the living room? I should have gotten up and gone to my room. I wanted to cover my ears to avoid hearing Aunt Neila talk about her husband. A sense of shame enveloped us. He'd been in prison? Why hadn't Mom ever said anything? Not so much as a hint. Nothing. Why the silence?

Aunt Neila glanced over at me. I avoided her gaze and pretended to be examining the books on the shelves next to the sofa. I couldn't even read their titles. The letters were swirling in my head. I'd forgotten every bit of Arabic I had learned. My mind could only focus on one thing. Uncle Mounir in prison. What had happened? Neila continued to look at me with those sad eyes of hers. She wanted me to stay. I could tell. She didn't want to hide a thing from me. Her wounded eyes bore into me, but I avoided them.

"I promise you, Nadia. If anything happens, I'll do all I can to find an airline ticket and send her back to you." She hesitated for a few seconds. "That's it — she'll be on her way back to you, there in the cold. But for the time being, she's just fine at our place, isn't that so Lila?"

I struggled to smile, pretending that everything was normal. But my head was spinning. "Sure I'm fine," I muttered. "Tell her not to worry about me. I'm not a kid anymore!"

Aunt Neila smiled. "Don't worry, sweetie. Call me more often. You know, it does me a world of good to hear your voice. *Bi slama ya aziziti*, bye-bye, Nadia."

I imagined my mother's voice carried by fibre-optic cables beneath the ocean, dissolving, and then, total silence.

I rushed to get up, to disappear and take refuge in my room. To run away from Aunt Neila's gaze, to run away from the truth. I didn't have the courage to look at her one more time. But she cut me off.

"I know you're upset by what you just heard. But

it's the truth. And truth always catches up with us, doesn't it?"

"Yeah," I said, trying to downplay the situation. "I didn't mean to eavesdrop on your conversation. I'm really sorry."

She frowned. "Sorry? Why should you be sorry? For hearing the truth? There's nothing to be ashamed of. Yes, I admit it. Nadia, Mounir, and I never told you about his arrest, about the seven years he spent in prison. Not because we were ashamed of the past, but because we felt you were too young, and we didn't want to frighten you."

Aunt Neila's frankness swept through my body and startled me. Slowly my embarrassment melted away.

"But why prison? What did he do? What crime did he commit?"

"The crime of helping others to escape from oppression. The crime of opposing the regime and of fighting injustice."

That did it. My curiosity was off and running now. "Was Uncle Mounir a political prisoner, like Nelson Mandela? Is that what you mean?"

Aunt Neila smiled faintly and shook her head. "Yes . . . No, not really like Mandela. No comparison with the significance of Mandela's struggle. Let's just say that he paid a high price for loving his country, for dreaming of a better life for the people."

I thought back to Uncle Mounir's strange words. The sarcastic, almost bitter way he spoke of the rich. I'd interpreted his words as jealousy or envy, but suddenly they took on a new meaning. I had unjustly accused Uncle Mounir of jealousy, judged him without really knowing him. Now all I wanted was to make amends. How they must have suffered! Years of happiness gone up in smoke!

Aunt Neila sensed how upset I was. She quickly got ahold of herself. "Don't worry your head, my little Lila. Don't feel guilty. It's God's will. There was nothing we could do."

I couldn't understand her reaction, her fatalism. I declared, "Excuse me, but there's nothing wrong with opposing an authoritarian regime. God certainly did not want Uncle Mounir to go to prison. It's pure injustice!"

Surprised by my sudden and unexpected outburst, Aunt Neila stared at me, mouth agape.

I went on: "It's true, I don't live here, and I only came to Tunis to improve my Arabic and get to know my roots under pressure. I'm not out to change the world, not to get involved in politics either, but that doesn't mean I have to accept injustice. In fact, I don't believe injustice belongs to any particular race or skin colour. As soon as you see it, you have to denounce it, and not justify it. Even if you're a believer, you can't accept injustice like something that's ready to fall on our heads at any minute."

Aunt Neila came up to me, her eyes shining. For an instant, I felt that she was about to speak, to tell me that she disagreed and explain that we had to suffer in silence. She held still, motionless in time. My hands were shaking. I wanted to stop them so they would not betray me. She kissed me gently on the cheek, and then took me in her arms. I could feel the beating of her heart like an echo in a deserted valley. Faint at first, then stronger. One, two, three seconds. Her rhythmic breathing rocked me gently.

She whispered: "You're right, little Lila, how right you are! If only I could put the past behind me."

∏ I ∏ E

Tunis, January 5, 1984

Neila wouldn't accept it at first. She refused to believe that Mounir could be a militant, that he could have taken part in the riots of the last few days. It was hard for me to accept too, but in another way. I'd immersed myself in the innocence of the years gone by to escape the new reality of my life. But now images were whirling in my head. Najwa had gone back home. Her mother had come to pick her up. Alone in my room, I thought about the happy moments of my life. How desperately I wanted to hold on to them.

I saw myself, heart pounding with delight, eyes sparkling with excitement, as Neila and I watched the cars and taxis rush through the narrow streets. We were riding a bus, a rickety, shimmying old white-and-yellow bus that spewed out thick clouds of smoke. The worn-out seats and the trash on the floor meant nothing to us. We were intent on one thing and one thing only. To see the new French film that all our classmates were talking about: *La Boum*. At first, Father didn't want me going to the movies.

"There are always a lot of hoodlums loitering in front of the movie houses," he said, looking me in the eye.

We were eating our evening meal around the dinner table: vegetable soup and quiche. A few slices of onion were floating in my soup. I hated onions. With the tip of my spoon I tried to push them to the side of the bowl. But with the slightest movement of the spoon, they slid back into the broth. I had a lump in my throat. It was hard to tell whether the onions or Father's outburst had thrown me into this state.

Finally, Mother let out a sigh, and turned to him. "What of it? There are hoodlums everywhere. Can you name one place in Tunis where there aren't men who harass women, who stare at them and make obscene remarks?"

I blushed. Sometimes, I couldn't really understand Mother's outspokenness. But this time, her attitude encouraged me, and I insisted: "Papa, please, let me go. All my friends have been. Neila and I are the only ones who haven't seen the movie."

I was lying. I wasn't certain that all my schoolmates had seen it, but I did know that Neila and I wanted to see it together. In the meantime, I'd forgotten about the onions; I was swallowing them without a second thought.

Papa knew he was losing the battle. With Mother and I against him there was nothing he could do.

"Alright, you can go. But on one condition. I'll come to pick you up at the end of the film. What theatre is it playing at?"

"The Colisée!" I exclaimed, my voice filled with excitement.

I could read the satisfaction on mother's face. Father had finished his meal; he washed his hands in the kitchen sink and then retired to the living room, where his armchair waited for him.

At top speed I finished off the rest of the quiche and washed it down with a glass of water.

TWO DAYS LATER we were on our way to see the film; the posters had been plastered all over town. They showed a smiling teenage girl slow-dancing with a boy, whose back was to us. The photo was located in the "O" of the word *boum*. I knew what *boum* meant. Not too long ago, Sonia had organized a dance in her parents' garage. To our surprise, she invited us — Neila and I didn't know why. We went. And of course, we didn't breathe a word to our parents. Outside, boys and girls were smoking. Inside, it was dark. I couldn't see. Kids were dancing to the driving beat of American pop songs.

Breaking away from me, Neila joined the dancers, which made me feel even more like an outsider. Neila was moving every which way; she waved for me to join her. I shook my head no. From the ceiling above the dancers hung a mirrored disco ball, flashing light across the garage walls. Now and again, I could make out familiar faces. Slowly I backed up and stepped outside. There I was, with the group of smokers. I'd extricated myself from a weird situation, and here I was in an even weirder one. In spite of myself, I smiled. That was my way of masking my embarrassment, of forgetting how ill at ease I felt, and how much I really wanted to leave. A few moments later Neila joined me. Her cheeks were flushed; she was almost panting. How ridiculous she looks, I thought to myself. Her clothes—that green blouse and the pleated skirt—were totally out of style. All the other girls were wearing the latest look: leather jackets, moccasins, Burlington socks, and miniskirts or pre-washed Levis jeans.

She wanted to stay; I wanted to leave. Her eyes avoided mine. Neila never looked me in the eye when she was upset with me.

The group of smokers who'd been standing beside

us went back into the garage to dance. Loud laughter ripped through the silence that had fallen between Neila and me.

Neila stayed; I went home. But the next day we walked to school and all had been forgotten. Our disputes were ephemeral, like raindrops in the Sahara.

WE'D ALMOST REACHED the city centre. Only one stop to go. Suddenly, the driver slammed on the brakes, throwing the passengers forward. We slid from our seats and almost toppled over.

The driver opened his window quickly. "Stupid bastard, you almost hit us!" he yelled at the driver of a Fiat that had come to a stop alongside us.

All the passengers were on their feet. A knot of them congregated around the bus driver, praising his quick reflexes and driving skill. People were talking in loud voices, gesticulating. Eyes were shining, tongues were loose, elbows were rubbing, odours were mixing. Everyone had a suggestion to offer.

"Why not take that crazy driver to the police station," one passenger offered.

"For two cents I'd punch him out. He needs a lesson in good driving!" shouted another.

An elderly lady in a *safsari* was gripping the cloth between her teeth. The rest had slipped down her shoulders, revealing an old worn dress. She couldn't stop praising God and the skilled bus driver. "May God protect you, my lad, may God bless you for saving our lives, may God preserve you for your children..."

She continued to declaim her prayers while readjusting her *safsari*. Other voices joined in, shouting in agreement. Neila and I couldn't figure out what had happened. A husky man emerged from the Fiat. He was fuming. The two men stared at one another, like cocks about to fight. Our bus driver got up, the passengers massed around him to form a protective shield. Neila and I were shaking. We glanced at one another, and while those fine people were spoiling for a fight we slipped out the back door that, by some miracle, had remained wide open.

Once we got off the bus we began to run, not bothering to look behind us. We had no idea whether the crowd had beaten up the driver of the Fiat. Nor did we care. We wanted to see *La Boum*. Luckily for us, the movie theatre wasn't too far away. We had to make our way along a section of Avenue Bourguiba to reach the Colisée shopping centre where the theatre was located.

"What time is it?' Neila asked me halfway there.

"Ten to three. We've only got ten minutes until the film starts."

It must have been quite a sight, two teenage girls running headlong down the city's major thoroughfare.

Passersby stared at us incredulously, shaking their heads with a look of disapproval.

Finally, gasping, choking, on wobbly legs, we reached the Colisée box office. Inside, the lights had already dimmed. The commercials flashing across the screen at full volume reassured us.

"We won't tell Papa a thing about the bus incident," I whispered to Neila.

"Are you crazy or what? You know me — I'm not a snitch. I won't breathe a word, I promise!' she responded, a big smile on her face. She'd already forgotten our misadventure.

But the excitement had just begun.

SOPHIE MARCEAU, THE star of the film, her friends, and her parents, transported us to another world. The film's romantic music, and the kisses exchanged by young people from another culture, another world, swept us away. Could we feel those emotions for a boy? I felt like Sophie Marceau, a heroine longing for love and adventure.

Papa was waiting for us outside the theatre. He was wearing his brown topcoat and carrying an umbrella. His features were strained. I spotted him as soon as Neila and I came through the door and we were about to make our way down the handsome marble steps.

He waved to us without so much as a smile. His face was indifferent, closed. A group of young men came out after us. They were *zoufris*, hoodlums, as Papa called them. They were chewing on *glibettes*, salted sunflower seeds, whose black pods they cracked and spat out with a single rapid and accurate movement. Neila stared at them. I lowered my eyes to avoid my father's, as he looked out of the corner of his eye.

"So, how was the film?" he asked in a monotone.

"Terrific!" we piped up in unison.

"We really loved it," Neila added.

Papa said nothing more. He was still watching the group of young men as it dispersed nosily.

"Uncle Ali, you studied in Paris. Is it as beautiful as in the film?"

"Paris was magnificent in my day. Now, I don't know. It's probably still as beautiful!" Father fell silent.

I said nothing. Neila teased me, pointing to one of the boys in the group.

"Look at that guy over there. Don't you think he looks like Vic's buddy?"

I nudged her hard with my elbow. I was afraid Papa would hear.

Neila could barely hold back her laughter. *Dreams are my reality* . . . I hummed the chorus of the music from the film. I remembered a few words, but my singing was off-key.

"So now you're singing in English?" asked Neila, in a derisive tone.

It was dark outside. The lights shone on Avenue Bourguiba. A few raindrops began to fall. Papa was walking beside us; he opened his umbrella. He didn't suspect a thing. His world was in order and ours was of no concern to him. We weren't little girls that he had to protect from the insolent eyes of the *zoufris* any longer. We were adolescents, bubbling over. We wanted to know everything there was to know, up to and including the *zoufris*.

TEN

Tunis, December 11, 2010

AFTER I FOUND OUT that Uncle Mounir had spent seven years in prison, my life in Tunisia wasn't the same. His sad story haunted me. I couldn't leave the city before learning more about his past, but I also wanted to discover the truth about my mother and Aunt Neila. Why did they arrest him? What had happened in prison?

I was a little ashamed of my egotism and the superficial life I'd been leading for the past two weeks. I'd been looking down on the people around me. What could I really learn from these people, from this country? Learning Arabic was the main reason for my being here, but I didn't feel like I was making any real progress. My instructor at the Institute for Living Languages was the most boring and the most tedious I'd ever encountered. He would pronounce a word, then smile. *Kitab.* Smile. *Tawila.* Smile. And so it went, until the end of the lesson. By the time the class was over, I'd so had it with those smiles that I felt like sitting down and crying for the rest of the day. When we broke up into smaller groups to practise the words we'd learned, I'd end up with other girls, mostly from Germany. They'd come to Tunisia for thrills, for a good time with strong vigorous young men. And a lot of cheap sex. Kill two birds with one stone was their strategy: learn a language and have fun. As for fun, they got all they could handle. That's what we talked about during class. They regaled me with their countless affairs. We talked in English. Monsieur Latif's knowledge of English was rudimentary, certainly not good enough to understand what we were talking about. When he came over to check on our group, we pretended to be practicing the words we'd just learned: *"Ana uhibu al lughat al Arabiya,"* parroted Wenda, one of the girls in my group.

"That's it; very good." I said to myself. "Our little Wenda just loves Arabic." Most of all she loved the trash talk and the swear words her Tunisian boyfriend taught her, the ones she repeated, laughing, whenever we worked as a group. Monsieur Latif was still smiling. He was proud of Wenda's efforts!

I didn't breathe a word to Mom or Aunt Neila. Instead, I would tell them everything was fine, that I was enjoying my courses and making good progress. Truthfully, I was learning more about the German girls' sex lives than about literary Arabic. But there was no solution. How could I drop out of the institute? What would I tell Mom? She'd be so upset and disappointed. So, every morning I went off and pretended to learn.

Meeting Donia, Jamel, and their friends changed my outlook and gave me a good excuse to do something else. In a few days with them, I'd learned more words and local expressions than in the weeks with Monsieur Latif. True enough, I wasn't learning the rules of grammar, but at least I was speaking only in Arabic. When I didn't catch an expression, Donia also proved to be an excellent interpreter, just like at our first meeting in the café by the lagoon. I was surprised. Today, she invited me to her place. But I was a little leery in spite of my enthusiasm.

"What do you think Aunt Neila? Should I go to Donia's place?"

That was only a few days after the telephone incident, when I'd learned a little about Uncle Mounir's past. The wound was still raw. Aunt Neila was getting ready to go shopping, standing in front of the door to the apartment, a basket in her hand and a shopping bag slung over her shoulder. She was wearing an olive-green raincoat. I noticed a broad streak of white in her black hair. Funny, I'd never noticed her white hair before she'd told me about Uncle Mounir's imprisonment, about injustice and about politics. Time slipped by stealthily. Tunis had taught me that much. Aunt Neila had applied kohl to her eyelids. The black only brought out the sadness in her gaze. I could see it flickering in her eyes.

"Why not? What are you worried about?" she answered with her customary simplicity, as if nothing had happened.

"I'm not afraid of going to her house, I just don't want to make a mistake," I stammered.

She raised her eyebrows, startled by my answer. "You are going to make mistakes. Me, I've been making mistakes all my life. Your mom too. Don't be afraid, Lila. Everything will be fine, you'll see."

Then she smiled at me, opened the door, and hurried off. I stood there, shaken by what she'd said. This wasn't the same Aunt Neila, the one who always cautioned me to avoid people in the street. No, this was a woman who was encouraging me to break out of my shell and step into the real world.

When I reached Donia's, the gatekeeper opened the front entrance. He was a much older man, dark skinned, with a burnouse thrown over his shoulders. His was a face caressed by the sun and the rain — a furrowed brow, furrowed cheeks, furrowed hands.

The aura of wealth that emanated from the place took my breath away.

"Come this way," he said. With an accent I could barely understand. "Madame Donia told me you were coming. This way."

He closed the high, white, sheet-metal gate as he continued to talk to me. He adjusted his burnouse, which had slipped to his left side. I followed him timidly.

The garden was being prepared for winter. Tall clay pots planted with fat-leaved succulents lined the front walk like sentinels. The walkway was white, spotless, and gleaming. At the far end was a massive broad wooden door. The gatekeeper pressed the doorbell and in a few seconds a young lady opened the door. She was wearing an apron similar to those worn by maids in the old films we'd see on television.

"Good morning, Am Salem. Wait a minute and I'll call Madame Donia."

I found it ridiculous that everyone used the word "Madame" when they spoke about Donia, as if she were a much older woman. I turned around and noticed, to my surprise, that Am Salem, the gatekeeper, had vanished. He must have returned to his sentry box. I stood in the vestibule of that beautiful house, a bit dazzled. The girl in the white apron hurried off to call Donia. I was stunned at the sight of so much wealth, of such luxury. Chandeliers dangled from the ceilings.

Gold-framed mirrors hung from the walls. An antique chair stood in one corner, a rosewood chest in another. What would Uncle Mounir think if he were to see me in this house, talking to the people who live here? I promised myself to ask him the question that evening.

I heard footsteps coming toward me. Donia. The one everybody calls "Madame." She threw her arms around me.

"How happy I am to see you, sweetie! How are you?"

"I'm fine. You?"

Suddenly Donia's face seemed to lose its colour, her eyes to glaze over. I hadn't seen her in a mood like this since I first met her.

Carried away by curiosity, I ventured: "What is it? Some kind of trouble?"

Donia put her finger to her lips, as if to instruct me to be silent. Then she looked to her right and to her left to make sure that no one was listening. She drew nearer to me, and took me by the shoulder.

"Come to my room," she whispered.

Her pallid face and her strange behaviour gave me goosebumps. My curiosity was growing. I followed her into the house, which looked like a palace straight out of *One Thousand and One Nights*. Chandeliers, art, and statuettes graced the walls and the corners. It was as if I was strolling through a museum. Donia opened a wooden door engraved with arabesques.

"This is my room."

I found myself in the middle of the Disney film *Aladdin*. A bed fit for a princess occupied the middle of the room. Curtains of white muslin cascaded from the ceiling. Donia sat down on a light pink velvet sofa and pointed me to a fine matching chair. I sat down without saying a word.

"This is my realm," she whispered, looking a bit calmer now.

"It's so pretty and so original!"

I was still looking around admiring the feeling of serenity her room gave me. Her eyes were shining; she was pleased with the compliment.

"Thanks," she said in a low voice, "that means a lot. Especially when it comes from a Canadian, like you."

I blushed, but Donia didn't even notice. Eyes half closed, she continued: "Do you know why I wanted you to come to my place, Lila, and especially here, in my room? Because I see in you the kind of goodness and innocence I don't find in my friends in this country. I feel I can trust you. You don't know the prejudices of this society. The rich on one side, the poor on the other, and the weight of tradition pulling us down into the past."

Donia hesitated for a few seconds, searching for the right words, her forehead showing a concern that I hadn't noticed before, and then she picked up where she'd left off: "I trust you like a sister. You're like the sister I never had."

My heart began to beat harder. I didn't know whether to be pleased with Donia's confession, with the confidence she showed in me, or to be nervous about the responsibility she was putting on my shoulders. Wasn't it a considerable duty to be the confidant or the sister of someone I'd known for only a few days?

"You saw Reem and Farah? The way they were behaving in the café the other day? Believe me, what I'm telling you isn't gossip or something I made up. But I can't hide it from you: they don't understand anything about life. They're big zeroes, all they care about is boys, the latest fashion, and keeping up appearances. So much the better for them! It's their right, you say. So be it. But me, that's not what I want. I want to get to the bottom of things, to talk about politics, about ideals, to reach out to people, to understand, to ease their pain. And you, you're just the opposite of those girls. I'd like to offer you my friendship. I'd like for us to do things together."

Motionless, I looked at Donia. "Thanks, Donia, for your kind and sincere words, but I really don't understand what I could possibly do here, in a country I barely understand, with people who are always taking me for a foreigner. I don't have a clue about Tunisian politics."

She smiled a smile of gentle exasperation.

93

"Oh, don't be so pessimistic, Lila. You can work miracles! You can help me in my search for justice. You can join Jamel and me. We can change the world."

She stopped short, and pushed one of her curls back into place. Her face was glowing. The sadness of a few moments ago had disappeared. How was I to describe this new Donia sitting across from me? She wasn't the calm and generous girl who rescued me from Am Mokhtar any longer. Now across from me sat a strong-willed, self-assured young woman, ready to meet challenges head-on, a young woman extending her hand to me, offering a pact to sign. But deep down, behind her strength and her energy, I thought I detected apprehension. Like the loose end of a thread that always catches on the button of a coat.

"So how do you think I can help you?"

Donia smiled. That was the question she'd been expecting since the start of our conversation.

"Lila, look at the house I live in, these walls and the decorations, the fine paintings, the curtains, the fabrics, the furniture. All this luxury and extravagance doesn't impress me. It all belongs to my parents. It's their life, and they sweated blood to get where they did. They give me everything I need, and I'm grateful, but something's missing. Meaning in my life, the search for happiness, sharing with others, a sense of justice. Do you hear what I'm saying? Didn't you ever feel that way?"

She paused for a moment, then went on: "I want to help the people around me, I don't want to live in a country where injustice rules."

A torrent of ideas came surging through my mind. Donia was right. I'd always looked far beyond my home. I wanted something else, something my parents couldn't give me. But the poor? To be truthful, I'd never thought of them. And even less the poor people here around me. But how could you change the world? Wasn't it all pure idealism?

"It all sounds very nice, all these lofty emotions, but what do you really intend to do? This country is a mess. You think it's easy to change things? You want to get involved in politics, is that it? Maybe you'll end up in jail, like the blogger Jamel was talking about the other day. I just don't know. Aren't you playing with fire, Donia?"

Donia shook her head. "You're right—the whole country is going to the dogs, but what do you think I should I do? Stay at home and twiddle my thumbs? I could do it and my parents wouldn't say a word. I'd be like everybody else."

She paused for a moment, then continued in a low voice: "Jamel and I have started writing a blog. We make up stories. Satires. Articles that denounce injustice and ridicule this dictatorship."

Things had now begun to come into focus. An

image was dancing in front of my eyes. I could make it out more clearly now. Jamel and Donia were an item. The poor boy and the rich girl working hand in hand to get rid of the dictator. What a touching dream! But just where did I fit in?

I struggled to understand. "If Jamel is with you, what do you need me for? I've only got a few weeks left before I go back to Canada."

"Jamel is my hero. He comes from a poor family in Ettadamoun Township. I'm proud of him because he thinks things through. Other boys aren't so lucky. A lot of them are in the streets. The girls work as prostitutes or as supermarket cashiers or textile workers. The boys end up as peddlers or drug dealers. Some of them risk their lives at sea trying to get to Lampedusa, in Italy, and others become delinquents. *Zoufris*, if you get my meaning."

I couldn't move. My life in Canada had given me everything I needed. Peace and quiet. A home that wasn't as fine as Donia's but was comfortable enough. An education. A cold climate, one I liked, but also warmth. The warmth of my parents and my friends. There I could handle my existential crises, my doubts about who I was. Now, here I was in Tunis trying to polish my Arabic . . . well, mostly. But suddenly I'd learned about injustice, about corruption. About Uncle Mounir and Aunt Neila.

"Lila, are you still there? What are you thinking? My stories bore you, isn't that right?"

"Not at all. I was thinking about all these coincidences. Your story, Jamel's, mine, and plenty of others. I don't know how to interpret them. Maybe they're all connected in some way. But you didn't answer my question. How do you think I can help you, specifically?"

Donia cleared her throat and leaned forward to draw closer to me.

"As I said, Lila, something tells me you're not like the other girls. You can help me with online searches, writing articles, and sending out messages on social media to encourage young people not to put up with the status quo anymore. You can help me when I go with Jamel to Ettadamoun to give private lessons in math, French, and English to kids who are having problems at school. I'm sure you'd love it."

I looked outside. The French door in Donia's room opened out onto the garden. I spotted a couple of birds swooping across the sky. Climbing and diving, like the movement of my heart. My enthusiasm rose and fell. I had to leave, to be alone.

"So, what do you say?" Donia asked.

"I don't know, I'm all mixed up. I need to think things over. I'm a bit at a loss. You know, the real reason I came here in the first place was to please my mother and work on my Arabic. But for the last few days, I've felt like I need to find out whether I should stay or, on the other hand, whether I should leave as fast as possible. Should I be getting involved in this adventure? Is it really worth it?"

"Of course it is," Donia shot back.

I took her hand. We were like two little girls alone in the classroom, far from inquiring eyes. Tunis had embraced us. Suddenly I let her hand go and got up.

"I've got to leave."

"But I didn't even have a chance to offer you tea, or coffee, something to drink..."

She wanted to bring me something, but I restrained her.

"Thanks Donia, but I've absolutely got to go. It can wait until another time."

She smiled. This time she laid her hand on mine.

"Fine, another time," she said. "You'll be back, won't you?"

"I promise."

Once again, Donia seemed pensive. The same look on her face that welcomed me at the front door had returned. The excitement of a few moments ago had slipped beneath a thick layer of reserve and caution. In silence, Donia led me back to the metal door to the street. I felt her hand seeking mine. For a moment we stood there facing one another, hand in hand.

"I'll send you an SMS. See you soon!"

I heard myself answer, "For sure!"

The heavy door swung shut behind me. I closed my eyes for a second. I was trying to register every word and image of our strange conversation. A car sped by very close — a few more inches and it would have hit me. Imagine ending my life here of all places. I stepped back and snapped out of it. Then I set out briskly. I needed to get back to Aunt Neila's.

ELEVEN

Tunis, January 6, 1984

"And now that social peace has returned thanks to the efforts of the Tunisian people . . . and after these disturbances, we shall go back to where we began . . . just as before, with no increases in prices for bread, semolina, or macaroni . . ."

THERE WE WERE, all seated in the living room, eyes riveted to the television set. The black-and-white images flickered across the screen as if in slow motion. We were at the mercy of the weather, which affected reception. If the weather was fine, the picture was clear and bright, and images marched uninterrupted across the screen. But if the east wind began to blow, our antenna would begin to pivot, swinging this way and that. All the cardinal points—east, west, north, and south—seemed to merge into one. It wasn't long before the picture blurred, zigzagged, and finally disappeared, white on one side of the screen, and total black on the other. The sound came in fits and starts: "Today...done well... We...thanks..." I was seated straight up on my chair, fingers crossed on my thighs, ears straining to catch every word. I wasn't in the habit of listening to political speeches, but this time, it was different. My father sat to my left, looking depressed as he watched without saying a word. I could see the swollen veins of his hands. And Mother hovered vigilantly, ready to respond to each new word with a tirade of abuse.

"Flea-bitten old fox! Why are you even still alive?" she shot back at the sound of President Bourguiba's words.

As for Bourguiba, he couldn't have cared less about my mother and her lowly housewife's insults. He was the one on television; he was invincible, invested by a divine mission, or so he thought. The venerable father was speaking to his children. We were all his children. That's what they kept telling us: the Father of the Nation would speak to his children to tell them the good news. He was speaking of the bread riots and had just cancelled the recent price hikes with a snap of his fingers. "Back to where we began," were the words he used. For some people, perhaps, but not for me.

Back to where we began for the price of bread and

couscous, well, so much the better for the people. So much the better for Mr. Everyman and Mrs. Everywoman, for my father, my mother, their friends, those poor civil servants who could now fill their shopping bags with baguettes and couscous to feed their families, all the better for the workers on the rich men's construction sites, who could eat bread and drink Coca-Cola that burned their esophagus and caused them to belch noisily. All the better for the rich, who could save a few dinars and squeeze more out of their housemaids, their gardeners, and their drivers. All the better for these fine people. But not for me. This "disturbance" of theirs wasn't going to happen without breakage. This disturbance had opened my eyes to a reality that I'd been refusing to see for years.

This "disturbance" wasn't going to be painless. It wasn't about the poor against the rich or about bread instead of a piece of meat. No, this "disturbance" had hit me in the gut. Awakened something in me. It lifted the veil from my life, from my parents and my friends. I really didn't want to go back to where we began. Was I an egoist, a spoiled brat? I couldn't tell. But at that moment I took a decision: to keep the bread riots going every day of my life.

"Poor guy, that Bourguiba, he's not getting good advice," Father exclaimed finally.

"Poor? You call that man 'poor'?" Mother shot back.

"He's stuck fast to power like a postage stamp on an envelope. All he has to do is resign! Let the wind take him away!"

Papa stopped talking. He could never win against Mother. She sighed, then continued: "Bourguiba or someone else, there's no difference. At least the price of bread is going back down."

As far as Mother was concerned, that was what counted. That evening—I was sure of it—thousands of people reacted just as she did. Money, that was what mattered. How much did you make, how much was left over, how much you could accumulate? Dignity, equality, justice—all that was for the intellectuals, the philosophers, and the crazies. The little guys only wanted to eat, to live; that was all there was to it.

Najwa was sniffling again. She wiped her nose on her cuff.

"Don't do that!" Mother cried out with a grimace of disgust. "Use your hanky!"

"I can't find it," whined Najwa. "I think I lost it."

"Well, borrow one of Nadia's. Next time, watch what you're doing. Money doesn't grow on trees, you know. You think all your mother can do is buy, buy..."

Najwa bounded off to my room, as light-footed as a Saharan gazelle. She didn't understand a word of what Mother had told her. She was happy enough to spend another evening at our house.

Father sunk deeper into his armchair, like a ship sinking in deep water. Mother got to her feet and went off after Najwa. The story of the lost hanky was only just beginning.

There I was, sitting close to my father. I wanted to talk to him, to turn a new page with him, learn from him and really feel his presence. Not just see his ghost.

"Papa, what do you think of all this? The demands of the young people who are in the streets, do you agree with them?"

How diminished, how fragile he appeared. He looked me in the eye. I could feel his distress, his humiliation. Bizarre; I'd never felt it before. The "disturbance" Bourguiba was talking about had given me a new way of seeing.

"What do you want me to say? I think we're entering a new phase. Our country will never be the same again. I feel it, but I can't explain it." He hesitated, as though he already regretted the daring words coming out of his mouth. "Concentrate on your studies, that's what matters most. You've got an exam to write at the end of the school year. Don't let those things distract you."

Father had quickly slammed the brakes. Too bad he hadn't followed up on his first impulse. In the beginning he'd spoken to me as a friend, as he would to an adult, but suddenly he flip-flopped, back to his traditional role, to his passivity, to his world. A world that little

Nadia, as a child, might have been a part of, but not the young woman I'd become, the young adult searching for herself.

I went back to my room. My attempt had failed. My parents seemed more and more remote. Far from my way of thinking, far from my ideas, far from the questions I was asking myself, and far from my aspirations. A wall was going up. In fact, it had been under construction for years, but only over the last few days had I come to realize that it existed. I didn't know whether to demolish it and let the stones fall, one after the other, or instead, to add stones to the wall each day.

I'd found refuge in my classes, and of course there was Neila. But it wasn't the same thing. I needed my parents. Needed to talk to them about life, about politics, about my fears, the things I wanted to do. But that was asking for the impossible. We were saturated in banality, right down to the bone. It dripped from our hair, oozed from the pores of our skin and from our day-to-day routine. "Eat, sleep, and study" was my parents' unspoken advice. I'd understood it as a little girl and never called it into question. But that day, at last, I'd managed to sweep some of the dust away. I was daring to think differently—not to memorize the notes I took in class, but to ask questions, to understand, to figure out what was really going on. To find out why Mounir had gone off with the *zoufris*. Was he one of them after all? Who invented those categories, anyway? Society? My parents? The government? All of us?

THOSE WERE THE thoughts weighing down my mind. I shook my head from left to right, nodded vigorously up and down. I wanted to disperse the thick clouds that were gathering and blurring my vision.

I heard Mother exclaim to Najwa: "Look in your little bag. Maybe you'll find it there. Your mother shouldn't have to buy you another one, life is too expensive these days."

Najwa was sniveling harder than ever and piped up in a desperate voice: "It's not there, Auntie Fatma. I can't find it. I'm afraid my hanky fell out of my pocket the other day at school when we were playing 'elastic.'"

Mother let out a cry that was more like the roar of the lion I'd heard at the Belvedere Zoo when I was a little girl, and it terrified me.

"Why are you always playing 'elastic'? When are you going to grow up and mind your manners like a big girl?"

Mother burst out of the room without so much as a glance in my direction. Najwa was holding back tears and then, as soon as she saw me, she rushed over and threw her tiny arms around my waist.

In a trembling voice she asked, "Nadia, didn't you play 'elastic' when you were my age?"

I smiled at her and wiped the tears from the corner of her eyes. She sat down on the edge of my bed. Her nose was dripping. Mother was going to scold her. She was waiting for my answer, her damp little hand was stroking mine.

"I just loved 'elastic.' But I was no good at it. We played every day in the playground, at recess. One of the girls was the champ. I could jump as high as my waist, but no higher. But that girl, she could jump as high as her head and sometimes even higher — we called it 'the sky.' We stretched our arms up, and still she could jump through the elastic band. She was really super, nobody could beat her!"

Najwa's face relaxed, her eyes were gleaming like two candles in the dark. Mother's reproaches seemed far away. Suddenly she leaned over toward me, for fear someone might hear her, and whispered sweetly in my ear:

"Me too, I just love playing 'elastic,' and you know what, I'm letting you in on a secret: I can jump as high as my chest."

I laughed a nervous laugh. Poor Najwa, I had no idea how she would ever find her way. Her father was dead. Her mother was raising the children single-handed. The country was going to the dogs. I saw myself in the playground of my elementary school. It was winter. My fingers were red and swollen with the chilblains that tormented me all winter long. A rubber band about ten feet long went around my legs, and I stood there, straight. Neila, a few yards away, was standing just as straight, the other end of the rubber band around her legs. Looking one another in the eye, we made faces and burst out laughing. The hems of our second-hand checkered skirts peeped out from under our dark blue tunics. Neila had two long braids and spindly legs that looked like crutches. The tiny hairs on her skin stood up in the cold, and her red socks came up to her ankles. My hair was done up in a ponytail that swung back and forth in the wind as if shooing invisible flies. Every now and then I'd rub my swollen fingers.

The whole playground was filled with little groups like ours. The younger girls preferred skipping rope. It was like a competition. You'd see girls leaping into the air, then landing on their two feet or — sometimes — on the ground. The games lasted until the school bell rang out and we dashed off in all directions to get in line and march back into our classrooms. With a quick twist of the wrist we slipped the elastic from around our legs, rolled it up into a ball, and hid it in our school tunics. Every day the same scene would be repeated. Sometimes, but not often, we would stroll around the playground, arm in arm, or arms thrown over each other's shoulders. We told stories we'd overheard told

at home by an loquacious aunt or a sweet old grandmother, or furtively read in books left on bookshelves
by careless adults or carefully hidden under pillows.
We would stroll aimlessly around the schoolyard, our
worn-out shoes kicking up pieces of gravel that would
skip off to one side and roll along the ground.

Quietly Najwa came over and lay down beside me.
She was staring at the painting hanging from the wall
of the bedroom. It was a cheap, poor copy of Renoir's
Jeunes filles au piano. I'd gotten it as a birthday present
several years before.

"I really like that picture, Nadia," Najwa whispered
without looking at me. "It's like you and me. Maybe
one day I could play the piano like the little girl in the
painting."

"Play the piano or play 'elastic,'" I said, teasing her
and tickling her feet. "You've got to make up your
mind."

Najwa curled up in a ball, holding her feet to protect
them from my harmless torments. Her face was gleaming. In spite of her laughter, she managed to say: "Both!
The piano and 'elastic.'"

Suddenly Father's voice rang out, tearing us away
from our innocent games: "There will be school tomorrow, they just announced it on the radio. Hurry up, off
to sleep."

Our faces dropped. Najwa went to put on her

pajamas. Me, I had to review my notes. I hadn't done a bit of homework for two days.

I dreaded going back to normal already.

TWELVE

Tunis, December 12, 2010

OUR MINDS WERE MADE UP. I would be going with
Donia to Ettadamoun. After our conversation, I
hadn't been able to sleep. Donia's words had surged
into my mind, turning it into a battleground. Soldier
against soldier. Idea against idea. Belligerents meeting in combat, then returning each to his corner to
catch his breath before beginning all over again. I
stayed awake until before daybreak. From the loud-
speakers of our neighbourhood mosque the call to
prayer came loud and clear, and then began to fade.
Allahu Akbar. La Ilaha ila'Allah. The voice evaporated into the still dark sky. I could make out each
word, discern each syllable, understand each phrase.
Heavy now, my eyelids closed. My eyelashes meshed.

Finally my body lapsed into sleep. The battleground disappeared.

WHEN I CAME back to Aunt Neila's place after my meeting with Donia, I wanted to do only one thing: pack my bags and leave. Go home to Ottawa. Forget this complicated world. Seek refuge in the monotony of everyday life. How did it all happen? Should I continue to listen to my mother and allow her to guide my life? I should never have agreed to come here in the first place. I came upon Aunt Neila and Uncle Mounir in the kitchen. He was slicing a baguette while she ladled soup into pretty blue bowls.

"We've been expecting you," she exclaimed.

Uncle Mounir threw me a smile as he continued to draw the toothed blade of the knife through the bread. Slices were accumulating. He put them into a wicker basket. With the side of his hand he brushed the crumbs into a small cup, dumped them into his hand and sucked them into his mouth. Head thrown back, he swallowed the breadcrumbs and seemed pleased with himself.

"Come, sit down with us. We've got soup, tuna *briks*, and a salad. A Ramadan meal and we're not even in the fasting month! That's how it is. I don't know what to cook these days."

I forced myself to sit down at the table with my

mother's friends who had become my friends as well, my foster family. I was heavy hearted, my head spinning.

"What is it? You don't look your usual self," asked Aunt Neila, her face showing concern. "You seemed fine this morning."

Uncle Mounir had just put the breadbasket on the table. He stretched out his arm to grab a bottle full of a yellowish-green liquid.

"It's extra-virgin olive oil, natural, freshly pressed. A friend gave it to me this morning. It's from his olive press. The place is more than one hundred years old. I can take you there one of these days if you like. You'll see the mill-stones they use to crush the olives. The pressing mats, like round doormats with a hole in the middle. They've been doing it that way for thousands of years. I'm sure you'd really like it. In your country, in North America or even in Europe, they call it 'organic.' And they sell it dear. But a friend gave me some as a gift. Here, taste some on a lump of bread. You'll see, it's delicious."

I didn't know what to say, how to respond to this unexpected deluge of information. Aunt Neila piped up: "Leave her be! Save your history lessons for some other time."

I sighed. "No, no, I like to learn things. Except that I don't know what I should learn first. I feel like everybody is pulling and pushing me to learn more than I can handle about this country."

Uncle Mounir opened the bottle and poured a bit into a saucer. You'd have thought he was handling the most precious substance in the world. He dipped a morsel of bread into the green-gold oil. He handed the oil-soaked bread to me.

"Here, tell me what you think."

Aunt Neila seemed upset, but Uncle Mounir pretended not to notice.

"Is there a problem with your friend Donia? You told me you were going to see her. You weren't quite sure, isn't that so?"

I wasn't sure whether to pop the morsel of oil-soaked bread in my mouth or answer Aunt Neila. For an instant I looked at them, then decided to try the bread. It had a strong taste. An intriguing combination of fruitiness and acidity—a bit like Aunt Neila's kindness and Uncle Mounir's cavalier attitude. How was I supposed to react to the combination?

"Well, what do you think? It's miraculous, isn't it?"

I kept on chewing slowly. The opposing flavors dissolved one by one, like my ideas, which kept melting away, one after another.

"I don't know. Yes, it's good, but it has an aftertaste. Something strong and a little bitter left in my mouth."

For the first time, Uncle Mounir seemed disappointed. I regretted my response already. I caught myself quickly. "It's good, really good, but there's that taste..."

"That's the secret! The flavor of good olive oil is in that bitter taste. The authentic taste that people have been trying for centuries to get. Purity."

Fed up, Aunt Neila commanded: "The soup is getting cold. Now it's time to eat!"

After the bread and olive oil, I couldn't swallow a single bite. It was as if my throat was tied in a knot. There was a long moment of silence. I didn't dare look at my friends.

Then, slowly, Aunt Neila repeated her question: "What is it, sweetie? Are you homesick? Missing your parents? Don't you like your new Tunisian friends? Is Donia bothering you, or what?"

"I don't know anymore. I feel like I'm being pulled from all sides. I'd like to go back home to Ottawa. But I've started to like life here. Donia is really nice, but she's asking me to help her, and I don't know if I can do it."

"Help her?" they said, startled, putting their spoons on the table at the same time.

I saw the faint traces of soup at the corners of their mouths. Strangely, I saw Uncle Mounir's hand begin to shake. Did I just make the worst mistake of my life? I couldn't tell. But the family Mom had entrusted me to had every right to know. Especially if things began to get complicated.

"Help her in the fight against injustice, against the

dictatorship. With her blog, and in her work with the poor young people in Ettadamoun."

My hosts' faces froze. Uncle Mounir got up from his seat. Aunt Neila said nothing, and shut her eyes.

"Lila, would you come out to the balcony for a minute?" he asked.

I tried to make sense of their reaction. Did it mean that they were terrified of the regime?

"Okay, I'm coming."

I could still taste the olive oil in my mouth. Aunt Neila didn't move. She seemed far away. Her eyes were closed. It was as though she was meditating on the meaning of life.

With deliberate steps, I followed Uncle Mounir to the balcony. He slid the glass door open with a grating sound. Like a curious cat I placed one foot outside, then the other. A damp wind struck my face. I shuddered. It was funny; I felt reinvigorated. The cold refreshed me. The cold brought me back to Canada; I felt at home. Two wrought iron chairs and a table stood in a corner. There was an old metal tomato can filled with cigarette butts on top of it. Uncle Mounir always stepped out here to smoke after meals, and sometimes he would spend hours reading. I could see him from my window, which opened onto the balcony.

"Sit down," he told me. It sounded like an order.

I obeyed. Now I was getting really worried. I had

no idea what he was going to say. I wanted to call out to Aunt Neila. but I knew she would not come to my rescue.

He pulled up a chair and sat down, put a cigarette between his lips, and lit it.

Hands folded in my lap, I awaited the verdict.

THIRTEEN

Tunis, January 10, 1984

MOUNIR HAD BEEN ARRESTED. His younger brother, Mohamed, gave Neila and me the news. Neila and I were walking toward the *lycée* and we ran into him, school bag on his back, held in place by two strips of cloth like suspenders, his hands thrust into his pockets. His trousers, with large patches on each knee, barely came to his ankles. He wore a wool cap with a pom-pom. We knew Mohamed well. We often saw him sitting, legs swinging back and forth, on the back of his father's wagon, the one drawn by a donkey. His father went from one house to another to sell black earth or sheep manure for the neighbourhood's gardens. Once we saw him with Mounir. They were on their way to meet the principal of Mohamed's school, who

was insisting that he take private lessons. Mohamed
was always smiling—mouth half open, displaying his
tiny, yellow teeth. But that day he was walking like an
adult, head lowered, a look of shock on his face. His
innocence had vanished. He had become like everyone
else: resigned.

"How's it going, Mohamed?" Neila asked him. Her
voice was unsteady; she hadn't heard from Mounir.

Mohamed came up to us. His eyes were downcast,
as though he was looking for something on the ground.

"Really bad," he answered. "Really bad," he repeated,
shaking his head, not even daring to look us in the eye.

We halted. Neila put her hand to her heart. She had
turned pale.

"Why? What's happened?" she asked, grasping
Mohamed to keep him from taking another step.

Finally I could see his eyes. They were red. His
nose, too. He'd been crying. We should have guessed.
Mohamed was babbling incomprehensibly. I thought I
caught the word "police."

Neila was holding Mohamed's hand and looking at
him with searching eyes. I'd never seen her like this
before, not even when she talked about her father and
the violent blows he inflicted on her.

"Mounir?" she asked in a low voice. "What's happened to him?"

"The police came last night. Late. I was sleeping

with my brothers and sisters. Mounir was in the same room as us. He kissed me before I fell asleep. He even said: 'Don't give up your studies, no matter what happens.' I smiled at him and kissed him back. Then, all of a sudden, in the middle of the night, I heard loud knocking at the door, and mother began to cry out. I woke up. Everybody else had gotten up. Mounir was standing beside Daddy. Mommy was crying. I was shaking with fear. Then I saw a dozen policemen standing there, right in front of me. I don't know how they got in or where they came from. They had our house surrounded. One of the police, the biggest one—he must have been the chief, I think—went up to Mounir..."

Mohamed stopped short.

Neila, her face distraught, eyes brimming with tears, begged him: "Don't stop, please don't stop. What did they do to him?"

Mohamed turned his head away in a movement of despair. He didn't want to look us in the eye. His mouth was twisted.

"The big cop grabbed Mounir by the neck. Then, right in front of everybody, he sla...he slapped him on the face. Daddy was begging them. There must be some mistake, he said. Mounir was not some petty crook, some hoodlum. He's a student, Daddy said. He's studying to become a lawyer. Mommy was crying, wailing in a loud voice. We were crying too, but quietly. One of the cops, a young one who must have been Mounir's age came up to Daddy. Like a dog he barked at him: 'You, old man, shut your mouth or we'll shut it for you!' And Daddy stopped talking, and Mommy too. I was so scared I peed in my pants."

"And Mounir, what did they do to him?" Neila asked, her words stumbling over each other.

"They took him away in the *baga*. When we went outside to see what the cops were going to do with Mounir, I saw three police wagons in front of our house. The neighbours were standing on the street too. Our next-door neighbour, Am Omar, came over to comfort Daddy. The cop who was holding Mounir just kept on insulting him: 'You no-good punk! You think you're a grown-up, a man? I'll give you a taste of how you become a man. You'll see.' Then the police went back into the house and swept up all the books that Mounir kept on his table, threw them into a sack and left. They were beating him, right there in the street. Mommy fainted. Lucky for her she didn't hear them cursing and insulting him."

"How's your mother now?" I finally managed to ask Mohamed.

"She was still crying when I went out this morning. She couldn't get out of bed. Hasna my sister is staying with her—she didn't go to work at the factory."

Without realizing it, we'd continued to walk. Now

we were only a few yards from Mohamed's elementary school. The pupils had congregated in front of the tall blue door waiting for it to open. Mohamed didn't want to talk. He fell silent.

Neila asked him: "Where did they take him? Do you know?"

Mohamed shook his head. His eyes avoided ours. Then, abruptly, he said in a near-whisper: "Daddy said this morning that he would go to the El-Menzah 6 police station. Maybe he can find out more."

Mohamed pulled one of his hands from his pocket and waved timidly to us. His school bag was still hanging from his back, as if all it carried was poverty. We continued on our way in silence. Neila was dabbing at her eyes with her hanky.

"What are we going to do?" I asked her, to break the silence.

"Nothing. I don't have the faintest idea. Do you think he'll get off?" she asked, eyes full of uncertainty.

"Sure, why not. He didn't do anything wrong."

"But can't you see? It's the police. The police! You think they'll let him go, just like that?"

I shrugged my shoulders. "So, are the police God, or something?" I was getting upset. Neila was giving up hope too easily. Sinking into despair.

"Yes, almost God," she shot back. "Mother told me the other day not to get involved with the police. She also told me to stay away from politics, it's for rich people. They're the only ones who can rule. People like us, we're nothing but *khobzistes*, we eat our bread and that's that."

There had always been a gleam of pride in Neila's eyes when she told me a story to show my ignorance. But this time, it wasn't like before. Hearing about people's gossip, their visceral fear of the regime, didn't impress me anymore.

"He'll get out, you'll see. Come on, let's get moving, otherwise we'll be late. I'm sure Botti will be watching, and we won't be able to climb over the wall."

Neila followed me, but she was dragging her feet. I didn't know what to say to her. She looked so miserable! She was suddenly another Neila, one who was ten years older. High-spirited, optimistic Neila, the girl who told me racy stories and taught me about sex, that Neila didn't live in the body that was walking beside me. I wanted to shake her, to wrap my arms around her, comfort her, tell her that Mounir would be released soon, that he'd been arrested for a noble cause. That he was no criminal, but a political militant, a dreamer who wanted to change his country for the better. But my mouth refused to utter the words.

We finally reached the schoolyard of our *lycée*. Very little had changed. And yet, the day of the riots I thought that the whole *lycée* was about to collapse. Aside from a few broken windows covered by pieces of cardboard held in place with tape, nothing caught my eye. The grey doors to the toilets, the acrid smell, the long corridors that seemed to go on forever, the paint peeling from the walls, the monitors' office dark like a tomb: everything was in order and in its place. The monitors were drawn up in front of the main entrance like rats, ready to attack, ears tuned and pointed noses sniffing the air. Botti, his potbelly overhanging the belt that made him look fatter still, was the ringleader. In one hand he held a whistle, and the other swung back and forth at his side. He looked even nastier than usual; his squinting eyes were two narrow slits. His cheeks were like two yellow potatoes separated by an almost invisible nose. Maybe he intended to get even with everyone who had joined in the rioting. Farther off, the students were milling around in the yard. The same old cliques, the same groups, the same laughter, the same exclamations. Nothing had changed. Our lives were returning to normal. But had they ever really stopped? We were back to where we began, just as we were before the price of bread went up. Neila and I wandered aimlessly around the schoolyard. Hand in hand, we strolled like ghosts among the living. We'd buried our fine memories and our indifference. Neila was prematurely grieving and me, well, I was boiling. Now I was questioning everything; I wanted no more of the futile and hypocritical

life I'd been leading. Heart pounding, I could feel change
rushing through my veins, blood circulating wildly.

In the classroom, our instructors' faces seemed fro-
zen in time. They didn't say a word about the riots. They
didn't speak a word about that day when the shouts of
the demonstrators invaded our schoolyard and drove
us out, panic stricken, not knowing which way to turn,
that day when the poor became kings for twenty-four
hours. That day when the coherent little world I'd spent
eighteen years building collapsed. They said nothing.
Not a word. Not a comment. Not a wrinkled brow.
Back to where we began, the Father of the Nation had
decreed, and his well-behaved children obeyed. We
sat down in our assigned seats, opened our notebooks
and our textbooks to the same page where we'd closed
them and thrown them hastily into our bags to flee the
melee. Flee the troublemakers. I was happy that Neila
was beside me, but every time I glanced at her, her eyes
were far away. She had set out on a journey in search of
a love lost too soon. Of happiness never consummated.

I couldn't stand the half smiles and half grimaces
of our instructors, their shrill voices when they told us
how to behave or how stupid we were. I couldn't stand
Sonia's mincing little routine, the way she constantly
made eyes at the Arabic instructor who pretended not
to notice anything but whose fingers were fiddling
busily in his pants pockets not far from his fly. I didn't

want to breathe the stifling, resigned, and nauseating stink that emanated from the class. My lungs cried for justice. And I wanted it right away.

My thoughts went to Mounir. The blows that Mohamed described to us that morning were now engraved on my memory. And the insults he so hesitantly recited were recorded like they were on a cassette that was playing and replaying in my mind. Slap. *No-good punk.* Slap. *No-good punk.*

"Mademoiselle Mabrouk, read the poem on page twenty-three, second stanza..."

Was someone speaking to me? I thought I heard my name. The instructor's words came to me as though in a nightmare, distant, muffled in cotton wool. I couldn't understand what he wanted me to do. Neila pointed to the specific paragraph in my open book. Then she gave me a light kick under the desk. At last I got it. The instructor was growing impatient; he opened his mouth to start making fun of me, but I cut him short and began reading in a loud voice:

Against my will, in this world below I emerged,
And my voyage is toward another world.
That too against my will, as God is my witness!
Am I predestined, between these two worlds,
Some task to achieve,
Or am I free my own way to choose?

I read the stanza straight through and a bit breath-lessly. The verses of al-Maari, a tenth-century Arab poet—pessimistic, ironic, and critical of human fail-ings—flowed painfully from my mouth. Better they had been left to rest in peace, and not mingle with the fetid air of the classroom.

The instructor, one hand in his pocket and the other holding the book, looked me over deliberately, then said: "What did Abu al-Ala'a al-Maari mean by these words? Can you please remind us of the themes we discussed in class last week?"

Three days ago I would simply have regurgitated the same banalities that we'd jotted in our notebooks. But on this day, I did not want to play the same old game. I held my peace. I did not answer. I was on strike. Neila's little kicks were getting harder. I ignored them. I heard someone whispering the words: "pessimism," "anger," "bitterness." I ignored them as well and stared straight ahead. Monsieur Kamel did not frighten me. I wore my insolence on my sleeve.

"Mademoiselle Mabrouk, not only do you not pay attention in class, but you do not even take the trouble to review your notes before coming to class, and you still expect to write your final exams in a few months' time? If this is not the height of negligence and lazi-ness..." He paused for an instant as if searching for even sharper words, and then cleared his throat and declared: "If this happens again, you will gather up your things and leave this classroom. I don't need any more dunces in my class. I've had it up to here!"

His face turned crimson. Fine drops of saliva sprayed from his mouth and onto Sonia's desk as she was rummaging through her school bag, pretending to look for something. She didn't even notice. Her aim was to pass with high marks. Monsieur Kamel would help her. Maybe he would even slip her the exam questions? Sonia could buy everything—why not an exam from Monsieur Kamel?

I did not lower my eyes, which irritated Monsieur Kamel even more. I was proud of what I'd done, and I wasn't going to back down. Mounir had shown the way; I would follow him.

The instructor threw me a look of disgust, then turned to another student. Now somebody else would bear the brunt of his rage. I was safe, at least for that day; after that, we would see.

Neila whispered: "What got into you? Why didn't you answer? You gave me all your notes the day before yesterday."

"I didn't want to. It's my choice. I don't want to talk to that hypocrite ever again."

Hiding her mouth with her hand, Neila did all she could not to laugh. I'd given her a bit of pleasure. That made me even prouder of myself. Too quickly she calmed down and sat straight upright in her seat for the rest of the lesson.

Later, on the way home from school, we walked in silence through the back alleys. It was dark, and light gleamed from the windows of the fine houses. The streetlamps were out, as the rioters had shattered all the bulbs.

Suddenly Neila said, "Nadia, was it Mounir's arrest that made you act that way toward Monsieur Kamel this morning?"

My eyes lit up; my body, which had become hard to carry, and my heavy hands were transformed by the few words Neila had spoken. She understood! She understood how hurt I was, how shocked. I knew it; Neila was my best friend. The smartest girl in the class. I felt myself coming back to life. I wanted to run all the way home.

"Yes! I did it to defy this rotten system of ours. I refuse to speak to that failure who called me a dunce. I don't want to have to look at that mug of his while Mounir is under arrest for revolting against injustice. The state pays our instructors to stuff our heads with useless information, to teach us better ways to keep quiet, and to put up with injustice."

"But where are you getting that revolutionary talk from?" she cut me off. "Is it that Karl what's-his-name who says so in his book?"

I smiled a bitter smile.

"Karl Marx, Neila. It's Karl Marx. Remember the name and cut the nonsense. But it's not him! Those are my own ideas. I kept them to myself because of my family, because of my teachers, because I was afraid to speak up, because of my egoism and my indifference. But you know something, what little Mohamed told us forced me to break out of my little bubble. And it was the thought of Mounir's face that gave me the courage to stand up to the instructor. It was the hope in his sad eyes that made me think, and think again. See what I mean?"

We stopped short, one facing the other. Two young girls in the darkness. From the distance came the barking of the watchdogs that guarded the luxurious villas. Those dogs would sink their teeth into anyone who came too close. But we were frightened no longer. There, facing one another, the tears streamed down our cheeks, we revealed our unhappiness for the first time.

"I promise, Neila. I'll never be the same as before. I'm ready to change the world."

Neila wiped away a tear; a timid smile fluttered on her lips.

"I don't know if I can change the world. But I'll do everything I can to save Mounir and to encourage you, my dear Nadia."

We threw ourselves into each other's arms. The

wind was whipping our hair; the dogs were barking louder than ever. We stood there, motionless. The couscous revolt had sealed our friendship, for life.

FOURTEEN

Tunis, December 12, 2010

"LIFE HASN'T BEEN EASY for me, understand?"

Uncle Mounir's eyelashes were fluttering. He was not looking at me; he was gazing into the distance instead, as if he was trying to bring the past into focus.

"I've been through too much. Ours was a poor family with five kids that had to keep moving from one place to another. No sooner did my father finish building a *gourbi* out of stone, brick, old scraps of cement, and sheet metal, than we had to build another. The police or the neighbourhood delegates of the Destourian Party would come calling and order Father to demolish the *gourbi* he'd just built. He did as they said, but started work on another one right away. Poverty moved in with us, became another member of the family. Until the day when a party delegate came knocking and made Father an offer. The government would give us a house, let's call it social housing, and in return Father would work as a day watchman for the municipality. The only condition was that he wouldn't be paid. It was their way of making him pay for the house we were living in. He accepted. What else could he do? It was like choosing between suffering less or suffering more. His choice was to suffer for us. My mother, my brothers, and my sisters were tired of always moving from one place to another, and even our animals—the few sheep and chickens we possessed—had had enough. So, rain or shine, my father sat on an old chair next to the entrance to city hall. His job was to report every day to the party delegate. He knew that he was reporting everyone's comings and goings, he knew he was a *kaouad*, which is what we call shills. Besides, I'm not even sure there was really such a job. And when he wasn't sitting right beside the entrance to city hall, Father took his donkey and cart and went off to sell manure to the people who live in the fancy neighbourhoods that had sprung up all around us. Time and again we had to move. The new residents had the money and the contacts they needed to buy the land and build their private palaces. But my father had neither the money nor the contacts. He spent his whole life between an old chair and a donkey cart. That's what poverty and injustice did to us."

Uncle Mounir stopped for a moment, then, still looking off into the distance, he went on: "I hated what the government had done to my father and one day, after I'd read *Capital* by Karl Marx, I swore that I would change things when I grew up. I wanted to spare my family the humiliation and the poverty, but I was too young, too idealistic."

His story excited me so much that I forgot my fears of only a few moments before.

"But you weren't asking for the moon, all you wanted was a little dignity, if I understand. What does that have to do with idealism?"

He looked at me for the first time since we'd stepped out onto the balcony, as if he was surprised to see me there. But just as quickly, his gaze shifted off into the distance once more.

"That's the problem. It's almost impossible to protect your dignity in this country. Asking for it is like asking for the moon. When one of my instructors began to lend me books by Samir Amin, an economist who specialized in developing countries, it was as if I could see the light at the end of the tunnel. I thought that my family's problems, and those of others like us, would be solved by a revolution. A social and economic revolution. 'Equality from the bottom up,' as we put it, so proud to use such sophisticated terminology. It would be a revolt of the poor against the mafia-style political power that controlled our lives. At university, I became active in the students' union. I wasn't one hundred percent Communist, and I wasn't one hundred percent Islamist. I was a hybrid. A dangerous and explosive mixture. For the police and the intelligence services at any rate. Nobody knew it, but I began talking with the workers on the construction sites not far from campus. I asked them if they wanted to improve their financial situation, to have medical care. They were young guys, seventeen or eighteen years old. They'd come in from the countryside, but there was no work for them in the towns and cities. There was never any serious agrarian reform in Tunisia. Every time they tried, it failed, and we ended up with more corruption, more young people unemployed, and more people leaving the land. The best they could hope for was to find jobs as apprentices on the construction sites that were sprouting up all over the Tunis suburbs and send their miserable pay back to their families in the village. I talked with them and encouraged them to set up a union, to unite against the greedy foremen and the contractors who paid them starvation wages and left them to sleep on the construction sites. No insurance, no social programs. Nothing. They had to make do with bitter black tea and a baguette spread with *harissa* to get through the day. Some of them would listen to me attentively, but most of them didn't want to hear a thing. One of them ratted on me to the police. You reach out a hand to help them, and they cut it off, and throw you to the lions, see what I mean?"

I couldn't tell what he was driving at. "Does that mean I shouldn't go with Donia and her friend Jamel to help the poor and denounce injustice?"

He did not reply; it was as though he hadn't even heard me. "The police came for me two days after the bread riots started in Tunis. I had comrades who kept me up to date on the situation in other towns. Tozeur in the south. Gafsa, where all the mines are. Me and other student unionists, we'd made up our minds to start demonstrating in Tunis. A lot of young people came out. We weren't expecting violence, but it happened. We were against the increases in the price of bread and semolina, but we were also against injustice, against nepotism. We wanted a fair chance for everybody. We wanted to alert the middle class about the way the poor were being treated. The unemployment. The humiliation. Whether we went to school or not, nothing was going to change for us. We were poor, and we'd stay poor. We were modern-day *Misérables*. The government ignored us. So did everybody else. But the young people of Djebel Lahmar, the 'red mount' — the colour of blood and of danger — from Ettadamoun Township, from Sijoumi, from Bab Souika, all the slums and the working-class districts, came out in the thousands when the unions sent out the call, but still more came out on their own. It was a cry of pain. A cry of despair."

I was shivering.

"When we found out that the government had reversed its decision on the price of bread, my comrades and I could barely contain our joy. We were shouting like madmen. But that very evening the police came to pick us up, one by one, like mice in a trap. They slapped us, they beat us, threw us in prison. That's what happens to revolutionaries. To people who try to change the world."

"How long were you in prison, Uncle Mounir?"

He rolled up his shirtsleeve and showed me his scar. It was like a snake eyeing me intensely. His skin had adopted a new texture. Time had done the rest.

"You see, Lila, this scar reminds me every day that you shouldn't try to take on the big shots, that even your union will drop you if you don't have the right connections. This scar shouts out to me that the police aren't choirboys, and that they won't hesitate to do what their superiors tell them, if not worse. I spent seven years in prison. It could have been ten, or twenty. What's the difference? The years don't mean a thing. Seven years, just think about it. My mother came to see me every Friday, a basket in hand and hurt in her eyes. Seven years for belonging to an unauthorized association and inciting the youth to violence. That's what they accused me of—I never confessed a thing. Even when they sliced the skin on my arm with a broken bottle I didn't talk. I let them do it, and that made them even more furious. At first, my father would come to visit me, but he died two years later. He was ashamed to work for the government that had confiscated his son. He never forgave himself. He was really hard on himself. They didn't even give me permission to attend his funeral. They told my little brother who came asking that I was too dangerous to be let out on leave, even for a few hours."

"And today, can you pardon them?" I asked, eyes moist, overcome by what I'd heard.

"I don't know. I'll leave it to God to deal with."

He stopped as suddenly as he'd begun. I wanted to comfort him, but I didn't know how. His story had given me the answers I was looking for, ever since I'd said goodbye to Donia.

What he told me set my bowels churning. It was the missing link in the chain of events that had brought me to Tunisia. Mother, fate, or God had brought me to this distant country. The idea was to learn Arabic, but there was another plan for me. A much wider plan, a more complex and subtle one. I'd met Donia. She'd asked me to help her in the struggle. And now I'd heard Uncle Mounir's horrifying story. What should I do? Back up? Go back to where we began, or start a new adventure?

Do as Uncle Mounir did? Or follow Donia, who turned her back on wealth for the sake of her ideals?

Uncle Mounir stood up.

"Uncle Mounir, I've got a question for you. I'm certain you're the only one who can help me. Do you believe I should help Donia with what she's doing?"

He looked at me long and hard. His scar was hidden by his shirtsleeve. The past had unfolded there, on his arm. Now it was gone. Obscured by pain.

"When I was your age, I followed my ideals. I didn't hesitate for a minute. Are you ready to do the same thing? I don't know. You have to decide."

I could not answer. Then, abruptly, he went back into the apartment, and I was alone with my thoughts.

FIFTEEN

Tunis, late January, 1984

I WAS MAKING MY way toward the *lycée* as laboriously as if I were dragging a ball and chain. Mounir's arrest shocked me, but not in the same way as it did Neila, who wept each time she saw me, that is to say, every day. I told her what she wanted to hear—the same words that I wanted to speak, in spite of myself. Mounir would be set free soon, I told her. He was a hero; he did what he did for the love of his country, like Étienne Lantier, Zola's hero.

"But this isn't France, this is Tunisia. Why would he do such a thing?" she asked every time I compared the two.

"I know, I know. Listen, Neila, France is the land of ideals, of revolution and human rights. Mounir was only defending the rights of the poor and following those great principles."

Neila fell silent; I thought I saw a slight smile stealing across her face. It wasn't her mouth or her eyes that smiled, but I noticed a tiny change — no one else would have seen it — and it made me feel better. It was as though her whole face had suddenly begun to glow, before everything fell back into place. Then, in a fraction of a second her expression darkened again. Like a winter day. My soul had grown darker as well. I didn't let on to Neila, and even less to my parents.

On returning home, I didn't feel like talking to anyone except, from time to time, to Najwa, my little neighbour, when she would come to spend a day or two at our place. Najwa was the only one with an innocent heart, the only one who didn't ask me questions, who loved me for who I was.

The pain I felt after Mounir's arrest also took the form of a near obsession with reading. First I read all the books on my father's bookshelves, and then I went off in search of more. At first, I registered at the library of the French cultural centre. But it wasn't enough. I needed a new challenge. Then — I don't know what got into me — I made a visit to the American cultural centre. Was it the feeling of inferiority whenever I compared my country with others? Was it the attraction of an exotic language? Or was it simply curiosity that led me to the centre?

The day of my first visit, I'd gone downtown with mother. We were strolling under the handsome arcades of the Avenue de France. Mother was looking to buy fabric to make a new winter dress. She'd barely avoided a fight with Father: we couldn't afford it, he'd insisted. Mother didn't back down. All her old dresses were worn out, she said. There was no way she was going to her friend's son's circumcision party in the same old rags. Father said nothing, and that drove Mother wild. She'd managed to borrow a little money in order to buy the fabric: our neighbour Hedia loaned her ten dinars because she'd received some of her husband's inheritance. Mother would reimburse her as soon as Father would talk to her again. I wasn't at all certain that Father would agree to such a deal, but there was no stopping Mother: she absolutely had to have that new dress of hers.

In and out we went, from one store to another. Mother badgered the salesmen on the price of fabric, where it was made, the quality of the thread. I couldn't have cared less about the conversation. The window of one shop opened onto the corridor below the arches of the arcade. I watched people hurrying by. It was cold, and they were wearing woollen coats, hats, and scarves.

"This one here is Dormeuil, made from wool imported direct from England," boasted the salesman as he proudly unrolled the bottle-green fabric in front of her.

Mother's eyes were focused on the fabric. She caressed the cloth with her plump hands and rubbed it in a slow, circular movement between her fingers.

"But it's too expensive. Make me a good price and I'll take two yards." She was almost imploring him, all the while attempting not to let on that she was dying to have that particular fabric.

The salesman, a portly fellow who made his way about the shop with some difficulty, pencil behind his ear, measuring tape around his neck, crooked spectacles at the tip of his nose to check the prices, seemed insensible to mother's supplications.

Distractedly I kept looking through the window. How badly I wanted Mother to buy the fabric and to deliver me from this suffocating situation. Mother pretended she was about to leave; she picked up her handbag and headed for the door. It was at that moment that the fat man said, with a look of resignation: "Alright, agreed. I'll give you a ten percent discount."

Mother turned and almost ran to the cash, a ten-dinar bill in hand. She rummaged through her handbag and pulled out another bill. I had no idea where it came from, but that was Mother: she had a solution for everything. The deal was done. The circus was over. Soon she would have her new bottle-green dress. I waited right outside the door of the shop for the salesman to wrap the fine fabric in coated paper and then slip it into a plastic bag. It was at that moment that I saw a group of young people a little older than me, maybe Mounir's age, entering one of the nearby doorways. I followed them with my eyes. It was the American cultural centre. Mother joined me, her face still flushed with excitement.

"Mommy, can I go and see what they have at the American cultural centre?"

She stared at me wide-eyed. Was I joking or was I serious?

I insisted, "I always wanted to go there and see what kind of services they offer."

Mother, overjoyed that she would be able to make the dress she'd dreamed about, granted my request. The truth was, she didn't really understand why I was so enthusiastic about the idea of visiting the centre, or exactly what I was hoping to do there.

"Fine, go. I'll be waiting for you in the patisserie next door. I'm starving. I'll get a quick bite, but don't be too long!"

I don't know what had come over me. Why, all of a sudden, the excitement? Why would I want to sign up at the American cultural centre? I hurried inside and began to look around. A woman in her fifties, her grey hair in a pageboy cut, with smiling eyes, interrupted my perusal of the premises.

"Are you looking for something?" she asked in perfect French.

Without a moment's hesitation I heard myself answering: "I would like to enrol at the centre to improve my English and learn to communicate in that language. I need to practise."

The woman smiled. Her welcoming attitude put me even more at ease. Slowly, I began to relax. She looked for a few seconds through one of the drawers of her desk, and then handed me a typed sheet of paper.

"Fill out this application form with all the required information. The registration fee is five dinars, and that's all there is to it. Then you can use our library and our language lab, where you can listen to talking books and practise your conversation."

She pointed behind and above her, to a kind of mezzanine. I thought I could make out the head of one of the young people I'd seen go by a few minutes earlier.

I rummaged through my handbag. I opened my leather wallet, which had a picture of a desert camel on it, a gift from Father. I plucked out all the coins, one by one. It was all I possessed. The woman kept smiling at me, showing no sign of impatience.

"Here you are, exactly five dinars," I said, handing her the coins. She took them without counting.

"On your next visit, bring two ID photos, one for

our files and the other for your library card, so you can borrow books and use our language lab."

I was quivering with joy. I don't know how long I might have stayed there; I'd all but forgotten Mother. Maybe she would make a scene if she knew I'd just spent five dinars in order to borrow books. But I'd made up my mind not to tell her anything. I thanked the lady profusely and promised to bring her the photos.

"What year are you in?" she asked me, unexpectedly.

I was taken aback. Why would a woman working here possibly be interested in me?

"I'll be graduating from the *lycée* in a few months. This is my last year." It was all I could do to get the words out. The woman smiled again.

"Good luck then."

How was I supposed to answer? Then, our English instructor's words came back to me.

"Thank you," I said, haltingly, and almost mechanically, added, *"very much."*

The woman waved her hand. Still surprised at what I'd done, I went outside to join my mother. It was the first time I'd spoken to a foreigner, an American, someone who wasn't my mother, my instructor, or one of my friends. "An outsider," as we called them in Tunisia. I was floating on a puffy cloud. My English was about to get better, fast, and I knew it. *I'll change my life*, I thought. *I'll become an expert in English.*

Mother was exactly where I expected to find her: in the pastry shop in the Rue Charles de Gaulle. She was standing at the counter, a plate of half-eaten pastry in her hand. Eyebrows knit, a severe look on her face, she spoke to me as if I were a child. Mouth full, she launched her attack: "You were there forever! What were you doing, anyway? I thought you'd gotten lost!"

But I didn't want to spoil my delight. I pretended not to notice a thing and answered her indifferently: "I signed up at the American cultural centre. From now on I can borrow books and read them in English, from cover to cover."

But even my attempt to control my enthusiasm displeased Mother. She made a grimace of disgust and shot back: "What are you going to do with English? Take a trip to the moon? Find a husband? Aren't Arabic and French enough for you?" She handed me a small package in white paper wrapping. "Here, a tuna pastry."

Mother could spoil anything if she put her mind to it. But I didn't even want to contemplate that. I took a big bite out of the pastry and swallowed my disappointment. The flaky pastry broke up into thousands of tiny pieces that came fluttering to rest on my blue coat. I flicked the crumbs away with my free hand and kept on eating the insipid pastry stuffed with a few chunks of boiled potato and a barely detectable amount of tuna.

"Finish your pastry! We're in a rush, time to go home."

With religious fervor, Mother was gripping her plastic bag in her hand. I didn't want to ask her where that other ten-dinar bill she pulled out of her purse at the last minute in the fabric store had come from. What difference did it make? Father would never know exactly how much she really paid for her new bottle-green dress. A quiet voice whispered to me that Mother had taken the money from the meagre budget Father gave her to buy our month's end provisions. Before long, we'd be eating only vegetable couscous and *lablabi* made out of stale bread and chickpeas. Thanks, Bourguiba. You knew what you were talking about. With one wave of your magic wand, you brought the price of bread and couscous back to where we began. Now, Mother could buy her fabric and show off her new dress to her friends. Thanks, Mommy, for your helpful hints and tricks for saving money for the things that really matter. So Mounir was rotting in prison for playing the hero — too bad for him. People were shot down as they fought for dignity and freedom? Too bad for them, too. Life had to go on.

I watched people entering and exiting the pastry shop, indifferent expressions on their faces. Everyone was thinking about his or her little life. As soon as they'd eaten their sandwich, their slice of cake or pastry, some of them wiped their fingers on the little scraps of greyish paper that passed for napkins and then crumpled them up in one hand and tossed them into one of the wastebaskets that stood at each end of the main counter, where most of the customers were standing. More than a few of those balls of paper missed the target, and ended their haphazard flight among the customers' feet.

The more impatient Mother became, the slower I ate. She made her way toward the exit, the plastic bag all but glued to her hand. With the scrap of paper that did double duty as napkin and plate, I took aim at the wastebasket. And like most of the other customers, I missed. Sheepishly, I pretended as if nothing had happened and followed Mother unquestioningly out the door.

For me, only one thing counted: being able to borrow books from the American cultural centre and immersing myself in another world to forget the one I lived in.

SIXTEEN

Tunis, December 13, 2010

TWO EVENTS HAD THROWN my Tunisian stay into turmoil: my budding friendship with Donia and the story of Uncle Mounir's shocking involvement in the 1984 bread riots and his years in prison. More and more, I felt that I couldn't go on as before. I wasn't the same Lila, indifferent and detached, looking on from a distance and observing in silence. "The outsider," as they called me here, who could care less about her mother's home country and who was visiting out of politeness, to make Mom happy. Uncle Mounir's suffering and courage had struck me right to the heart. Aunt Neila's patience and her almost limitless love for her husband had stunned me. And then there was Donia, her desire to change her country was crying out to me. She had money and power. She had a car, a house, servants who addressed her as Madame, and friends who looked up to her, and yet she had chosen another path. Her mind was made up: she would become a dissident, help the poor, the people who had no voice, the disinherited. Why? Uncle Mounir and Donia had become two great examples for me.

It's funny. Less than a week ago, I had been counting the days until my return to Ottawa. And now, here I was in Tunis, thinking about what I could do to help the people around me. Would Mom understand my sudden metamorphosis? Would she see a new Lila who was beginning to emerge from a cocoon? This was not a Lila who was doing better in Arabic, as Mom had so ardently wished, but instead a Lila who wasn't obsessed with her little problems. This other Lila had seen the pain of others, and it had opened her eyes to a wider world. Maybe she would understand me, maybe she would back me up; maybe she'd already taken that same path?

I made my first decision, a calm, cool, and collected decision, not for the sake of Donia or Uncle Mounir, but to help me find out who I really was. Today, I was convinced that in the few days I had left in Tunis, I would get to know myself a lot better and answer the questions that have been weighing on my mind. Who was I? What did I want to do with my life? Where did I want to go? I would never have believed that by coming to this strange, foreign, and sometimes bizarre place, I would be able not only to confront my longstanding fears, but also to overcome them.

"I accept Donia's proposal." I was startled to hear myself whispering my resolution, as if to prove that I was ready.

I picked up the backpack that was my constant companion, made sure I had my cellphone, and left the empty apartment. My aunt and uncle had already left for the market. They'd told me their plans yesterday evening. I heard their whispers and their muffled footsteps in the kitchen and the living room through the half-open door to my room. I didn't want to go to my Arabic course. I was striking out to discover the city with my own eyes. I wanted to reach my own conclusions, without waiting for someone else's approval or impressions.

Outside, the weather was mild. A pale gentle winter sun enveloped me with a layer of benevolence. I set off down the sidewalk — or, more accurately, down what used to be a sidewalk. Cars were parked one behind the other, every which way. The street, which was narrow to begin with, looked microscopic. I stepped off the sidewalk from time to time when I was unable to find a narrow space to squeeze through and made my way along the pavement. An oncoming car made me leap back onto the sidewalk. After waiting for it to pass, I continued on my way. My outing was like a video game: I had to get to my destination without being crushed by the obstacles I encountered en route: a car rushing by at high speed, a motorcycle zigzagging between cars, pedestrians like me seeking safe passage through the urban labyrinth. I passed by Donia's place on my way. The watchman, head swathed in the hood of his burnouse, was snoozing in his plastic chair in the warmth of the sunlight like a chill-prone cat. I tried to find Donia's balcony. The shutters were closed; maybe she was still sleeping.

Am Mokhtar was smoking a cigarette in front of his café. A girl in tight-fitting jeans—the cleaning lady—emptied a pail full of water as she pulled a squeegee back and forth in an attempt to clean off the greasy sidewalk. Cigarette butts floated in the soapy puddles. Am Mokhtar didn't see me go by. Either that or he was too intent on sticking his finger in his nose while sizing up the cleaning lady's behind. The voice of a sheikh reciting the Qur'an on a cassette or on the radio came from inside the café. I continued on.

When I got to the bus stop, an elderly woman wearing a traditional *safsari* was waiting there, holding a wicker basket. She nodded in greeting. I smiled back. Across from the stop there was a large shopping centre. I'd gone in to pick up some things a couple of times. The shops hadn't opened yet, but the saleswomen, wearing plastic sandals, their pants rolled up above their calves, were nonchalantly cleaning the storefronts and chattering noisily. Womenswear shops and toy stores rubbed elbows with pizza parlours and newsstands. Ambulant merchants were loading their pushcarts with toys, trinkets, manicure kits, headbands, contraband cigarettes, and packages of chewing gum. Some distance away, two uniformed policemen watched the scene as they chatted in low voices.

Finally, my bus came. The woman got on first. Her *safsari* slipped down onto her shoulders, leaving her greying hair uncovered. With a practised movement of the jaw she caught the fabric before it could slide any further. I bought my ticket and sat down on one of the seats that were still intact. The others were half-broken, wobbly, dirty, or had been ripped off. There were only a handful of passengers. Most of them stood. The old woman took a seat behind the driver. A pane of glass separated them, but it was as though there was no barrier, as if an ongoing conversation was starting up again. They must have known each other. I looked over my shoulder out the window. Swarms of cars were tailing us like wasps. Our bus came to a stop in traffic, then started off again.

That gave me more time to take in the streets, the houses, the buildings. I knew the route by heart. I took

it every morning on my way to my Arabic course at
the Institute for Living Languages. But today, I was
starting fresh; I would write whatever I wanted and I
would learn at my own speed. No more Monsieur Latif
and his smirk, no more German girls bragging about
their dates. That was all in the past. I thought about
Uncle Mounir's life in prison, about how his education
had come to an abrupt end. How could he survive so
much humiliation, so much injustice? How could he
stand straight, how could he live a normal life after
that? I found no answer to my questions. And why
hadn't Mom spoken a word about any of this? Was
she worried for me, for her friends? Why did she only
want me to learn Arabic when a whole swath of history lay hidden?

The more I thought about it, the more convinced I
became that I had to see Donia. I had to talk it all over
with her. She was the here and now, the face of the
country that was struggling to find itself. She was the
one who could help me get a better understanding of
people who lived here and maybe even of my mom's
real motives. I'd promised her an answer, and I intended
to call her today to talk it over.

The bus was driving down the wide streets of the
capital. The sight of rundown old buildings caught my
attention. How did people live here before? How did
they go about their lives? The clotheslines that waited

for the laundry and the pots of geraniums arranged on the balconies contrasted with the sad, gloomy atmosphere of the city. In Ottawa, the downtown area was clean, the office towers were tall and luxurious, and people were serious, conservative in their tailor-made suits as they walked along the sidewalks attempting to hail a cab or held doors open before stepping into a building to escape the polar cold of winter. The people here seemed resigned and unhappy. Sadness had become second nature, their way of life. It was a mask they put on every day when they woke up in the morning in order to go to work to earn their living.

There was a policeman at every corner. I couldn't understand what they were doing there. But there they stood erect, wearing the same expression as the rest of the population. Were they watching the birds flying high overhead? Were they thinking about their monotonous lives?

The old woman's cries brought me back to reality. I got up and approached her. Her *safsari* had slipped to the floor, revealing her plump body. She was wearing a flowered dress that came down to her knees. Her face was crimson with anger, and she was talking in a loud voice. A gentleman seated beside her was attempting to calm her down, and a girl held out a vial of Eau de Cologne to relax her. She took a sniff and said to the girl: "Ah that little bastard, that *zoufri*! Did you see how he pushed me, then grabbed my basket? And my purse along with it! Near tore my hand off."

She slapped her leg and looked left to right. The bus driver left his vehicle to give chase to the thief, who had already made good his escape and vanished into the crowd. I got out of the bus discreetly and continued on foot. The sight of the old woman in tears left me in a state of shock. I hadn't seen the guy who grabbed her basket. Why did he do it? I wondered. Maybe he was hungry or had a family to feed? But did that mean he had to steal?

The streets were swarming with people. I barely recognized where I was. Which way should I go? I wanted to take a few photos, walk through the streets, and then go back home. I passed a public park that was full of mature trees. A man who couldn't have been more than twenty was standing in front of the park's iron fence. In front of him was a pile of small paper boxes atop an improvised stand. He was selling cigarettes. Not too much farther along another young man was selling belts that hung from his open arms. The two men looked almost alike to me — there was nothing particular to distinguish them except for their expressions, which implored passersby to purchase the merchandise. The words they spoke to extol the qualities of their goods echoed in my ears. I turned away as soon my curious gaze alighted on them. The sight of their poverty made my stomach churn. A poorly clipped moustache, a broken tooth, sleepless eyes, a tattered sweater. I felt ashamed of my comfortable life, and of my tourist's attitude: once my curiosity was satisfied, I no longer knew what to make of these faces, of the outstretched hands of these people that I saw around me, in broad daylight, for the first time. What should I do? Look away or keep going?

People were hurrying along the sidewalks in all directions as I walked straight ahead, intoxicated by everything I was seeing. My mind was whirling. I didn't know whether to go back home or continue my impromptu journey through the city. I came out into a public square, where light rail trains, cars, and pedestrians fought for space. There was a tiny park that was almost hidden, and in the centre of the park loomed a bronze statue of a man wearing a cloak and a turban holding a large book. Nobody was stopping to look; everyone was on his or her way somewhere else. And all the while, the man in bronze surveyed the scene from his six-foot-high pedestal.

More impromptu stands, more uniformed police. A flood of cars and motorcycles was pouring through the streets. I approached the statue; carelessly, I walked right across the meticulously tended grass. No one was watching. I wanted to find out who this man was. *Ibn Khaldun, 1332–1406* I read on the marble plaque;

below, words in Arabic that I could not make out.

Who was this man? Everything I'd learned in my history courses had evaporated. *A scholar or an ancient hero*, I thought. I pulled out my camera, but a huge cathedral immediately to the left caught my eye. A group of tourists was posing in front of the steps. I was surprised. Mom never told me there was a cathedral in downtown Tunis! I crossed the street to get closer to the brown-and-grey structure. Beggars converged on me, hands outstretched, mouthing incomprehensible prayers. One was carrying a baby; another, legless, was seated in a wheelchair. "Never give anything to the beggars, they all belong to criminal gangs," Aunt Neila had often told me, each time I prepared to go out.

But today I couldn't look away from the poverty. I hesitated, then took some coins from my pocket and handed them to two beggars. They all but ripped the money from the palm of my hand, then threw me a quick "thank you" before vanishing into the crowd. Still overcome and astonished, I stood there, tense. Another group of tourists, their guide among them, was making its way in my direction. I attempted guardedly to catch a few of the guide's words.

He was speaking English: "The Cathedral of Saint Vincent de Paul was built in the nineteenth century. It opened on Christmas in 1897. As you can see from outside, this magnificent cathedral features several architectural styles: Moorish, Neo-Byzantine, and Gothic..." Listening closely, yet looking in another direction so as not to draw attention to myself, I picked up the guide's words, one by one. Like on an old record, their syllables rapidly faded away in the interior of the cathedral, as if sucked in by the soaring space. Cameras seemed to be clicking in unison, as their flashes flickered brilliantly in the darkness of the vaulted ceiling.

The sight of the passersby, acquiescent and indifferent, brought me back to the reality of the city. I continued, attempting to catch a crowded bus that wouldn't stop to pick me up. Then Avenue Habib-Bourguiba swept me up into its embrace. The trees that lined it were carefully trimmed, and the sidewalk cafés displayed their tables and chairs for customers who would pause for an espresso or a glass of tea in the brisk winter weather. It was almost as though I were back on Sparks Street, in the summer, with its window-shoppers and its diners thronging the open-air restaurant patios. Where had I been all this time? Stuck in the stifling lecture rooms of my Arabic courses or back at the apartment? Why hadn't I struck out to discover Tunis before, why hadn't I made an effort to discover its hidden treasures?

The ringtone of my phone shook me out of my reverie. It checked the number: it was Donia. I answered straight away.

"Hi Lila, how are you?"

"Fine! I'm wandering the streets of Tunis like a tourist."

"Lila, can we meet this afternoon? I really need to talk to you."

"Okay. Uh, Donia, I've got some news for you."

Silence.

"Donia, I accept your proposal, I'll help you. Starting right now, today, I'll be ... let's call it your assistant-slash-friend."

I heard a long shriek of delight.

"I just knew it! I knew it, Lila. Let's get started right away. I'm looking forward to working together. You'll see what we can do."

"Me too, Donia! I'm really happy to find out at last what brought me here."

She burst out laughing. "We've got to celebrate! This is the best news I've had for days now."

"It's a deal!"

We agreed to meet as soon as possible. I ended the call. An enormous weight had lifted. I felt relieved, as if I'd shared a great secret with a childhood friend. This was an enchanted city. It had bewitched me and was causing me to do things I hadn't even thought I could do a few weeks ago. What else did it have in store for me?

SEVENTEEN

Tunis, February, 1984

I MET ALEXANDER — Alex, for short — at the American cultural centre in Tunis. I'd stop by every Friday to read books in English, listen to cassettes in the language lab, or leaf through magazines that I had trouble understanding. Sometimes I would take a few minutes to relax on the comfortable chairs in the reading room, think about my life, and escape from Mother's orders and Father's silence.

Alex worked there as a computer technician, installing the first computers. His father was Canadian, his mother American. He lived in Ottawa. He'd gotten his job a year before, and had jumped at the chance to work in Tunis for a year. I learned all those details from our weekly chats. He smiled at me first; I was trying to

locate a book on the library shelves and mistook him
for a librarian. I had no idea how to go about finding a
book. I looked over all the titles and attempted to locate
what I was looking for among the dozens and dozens
of books packed in alongside one another.

"Is this where I can find...?" I asked him in a low
voice, so I didn't disturb the people in the reading room
nearby.

Alex had a Mediterranean look. I might have taken
him for a Tunisian if there hadn't been something dis-
tinctive about the way he carried himself. I could never
have imagined he was Canadian or American. In my
mind, an American was someone who looked like a
movie star, someone like Clark Gable, Marlon Brando,
or Rambo. Alex didn't look like any of them. He was
average height with close-cropped brown hair. His eyes
were dark blue, almost black. His face was oval shaped,
and he was always smiling, his shoulders broad and his
posture straight. His gentle manners contrasted with
his rapid step and serious expression. I spoke to him
in French the first time. I was ashamed of my accent
in English, but he answered me in good French, with
a hint of what I thought was a Provençal accent. Only
later did I learn that his accent was French-Canadian.

He pulled a book from the shelf in front of us and
pointed to the small sticker on the spine that indicated
letters and numbers.

"You have to find the right code to identify the book you're looking for," he explained.

I blushed. The young man had exposed my ignorance for all to see.

"Do you see that lady, over there, at the desk? I'm sure she'll be able to help you better than I can. She's the chief librarian. I'm in charge of setting up the computer system."

I recognized her; it was Mrs. Williams. She did checkouts and returns. She had a severe, almost intimidating appearance. And I was far too shy to ask her for advice. I wanted to learn myself. Clearly, my approach wasn't working. I wasn't as clever as I thought I was!

Alex intuited my reservations. "I can help you later, if you like, but now I've got to get back to work, splicing cables and connecting computers."

I stood there, taken slightly aback. He seemed so young, as though he were still a student at the *lycée*. The boys at school spent all their time talking about soccer, and making obscene comments about girls. Others kept quiet, and I never knew if they were unable to actually utter those insults or were just too well brought up to do so. Once, as I was about to talk to Samir, a boy in my class who was quiet and polite, and who sat behind Neila and me, I saw that he was staring at a photo of a nearly nude woman on one of the pages of his notebook. She was bare breasted and a microscopic string only barely concealed her most intimate parts. Samir quickly squirreled the photo away in his school bag, pretending nothing had happened. He couldn't fool me. I was disgusted. I couldn't look him in the eye. When I mentioned it to Neila during recess, she laughed.

"So, you think that all the boys are chaste like us little prissy princesses. They're exploring life, sweetie. All of 'em," she went on, tracing a semi-circle that encompassed the entire schoolyard with her index finger. "They've all slept with a girl or dreamed about doing it. The ones that don't have the guts or the means make do with porn photos, like that dimwit Samir."

"So how come you know so much?" I challenged her, hanging on to what was left of my self-constructed world of ideal romantic love.

"Mounir filled me in one time."

Now I was really shocked. Her frankness was beginning to irritate me.

"So, you've been talking about it with him!" I said, adopting my mother's censorious tone.

She shrugged, indifferent to my troubled expression.

"Sure, we talk about it, and why shouldn't we? It's perfectly normal, don't you think? We have to. One day I'll marry Mounir and I'll have children with him."

Neila was adept at shocking me and educating me at the same time. I fell silent, while she kept on laughing at my offended airs.

I promised myself I would never talk to another boy in my class. Ever since the incident with the daring photo, I couldn't even look at any of them. In my eyes they were all vulgar and crude. Unlike them, Alex, who seemed to be about their age, was so polite, so different. I felt drawn to him. I wanted to talk to him and ask him questions, as though I'd known him for years, but I did nothing. I waited until I saw him again.

I didn't say a word to Neila about my encounter with him. I didn't want to touch the open wound left by Mounir's arrest any more than I wanted to talk to her about something I couldn't make sense of, couldn't define. I didn't even know why I was attracted to this foreigner, who didn't even speak my language. The more I thought about him, the less I understood what was going on inside me.

THE CALM BEFORE the couscous revolt had reasserted itself. The dust had settled. My parents had slipped back into their routine. Neila stopped talking to me about Mounir. Only her gaze told me she was thinking about him. And in an attempt to forget, I did everything I could to avoid that gaze. The first signs of spring broke through the gloom that had settled in after the bread riots. Warm sunbeams proclaimed the early arrival of summer. The prospect reminded me every day that my final exams were approaching, and my stomach would tie itself in knots at the thought. Of course I wanted to do well, but I had no idea what I would do afterwards. Before the riots, I'd been a kind of automaton. I lived to study. But since Mounir's arrest, my world had turned upside down, and that obsession had evaporated.

I'd regained control of my life. I enjoyed reading and writing. I uncovered a real passion for English, a passion I never suspected. I read the books I borrowed from the cultural centre and went back to borrow new ones every Friday. I discovered writers like Steinbeck, Dickens, and Fitzgerald. Body and soul, I dove deep into one historical period after another: the Industrial Revolution in England and its perverse impact on the working classes; the Great Depression in the United States and the changes that followed it; the Roaring Twenties, with their taste for luxury, extravagance, and escapism that led to the dark years that came in their wake. I couldn't understand everything I read, but I loved the stories. Dictionary close at hand, stretched out on my bed, I spent hours savouring my newfound books and the new worlds they held out to me. My reading, and my visits to the centre, functioned as an escape hatch. Which did me the greatest good? The books I read or the sight of Alex? I couldn't say for sure.

He was immersed his work the second time I met him. When he saw me, he smiled, but unlike our first meeting, this time I managed to return his smile. He was working on the centre's computer system, coming and going from the main reading room and another room, which I glimpsed through the open door. The reading room was full of people. University students were talking endlessly about their final exams. I kept my nose deep in my book, but raised my eyes from time to time to look around. It was at such a moment that our eyes met. I immediately lowered my gaze and pretended to continue reading. But I wasn't concentrating on the page in front of me. What could he be thinking? Why had he come to Tunisia? Why did he leave his country and come here to work? How did people in his country live? As I was getting up and preparing to leave, Alex came over to me and pointed to something on the floor.

"I believe you've dropped some sheets of paper."

What a charming accent! I thought, almost forgetting to look down to the spot he indicated.

"Ah yes, right, they're my notes. I put them on the floor and I was going to pick them up, but I almost forgot."

In my excitement I kept talking as I stooped down to pick up my notes.

"Look, I totally forgot my promise to show you how to find books. I've got a few spare minutes today. Would you like to do it now?"

Mechanically I stuffed my scattered notes back into

my school bag and without a second thought answered in the affirmative. He seemed as happy as a little boy letting a friend in on a secret.

"My name is Alexander. I'm Canadian, I've been working here for the last few months, and next summer I'll be going back to Ottawa, where I live."

He spoke so confidently. What a contrast with my perpetual case of nerves. An ocean separated our two worlds, but two cultures were meeting now. Alexander gave me a detailed explanation of the codes that were used to classify books. He explained how the little file-drawers that held thousands of cards filed in alphabetical order would be replaced by a sophisticated computer system soon.

"For example, you enter the name of the author you're looking for and in a few seconds you see all the titles that match the name. Look, I'll give you a demonstration. Which writer would you like to read?"

"Fitz... Fitzgerald," I answered, stammering.

He looked at me, wide-eyed. I was afraid I'd mispronounced the name.

"You know, the one who wrote *Tender Is ... Is the Night*, if you can make out what I'm trying to say."

"That's F. Scott Fitzgerald alright—a great American writer. I really like him myself."

He sat down and typed on the keyboard, and then showed me the list of Fitzgerald titles.

"See, it's like magic. Here are Fitzgerald's other books: *This Side of Paradise, The Beautiful and Damned, The Great Gatsby.* Just before each title there's a code you can jot down and then find on the shelves."

I listened attentively. The way he pronounced the original English titles left me open mouthed with admiration. Not to mention his eagerness to explain things to me. Why was he so happy to show me his work, explain how to locate a title?

"Thank you so much for your kindness. You explained everything so well. Luckily for me you work here and could make it all clear for me." I could barely get the words out.

He interrupted me.

"But this system isn't available to the public yet. It will take a few more months before it's in service. I'm working on it with my colleagues, but it'll happen!"

"Don't give up! You can do it!"

"Thanks," he answered with a fresh smile. "You never told me your name."

"Nadia. Thanks. Thanks a lot."

I could feel that it was time to leave. I no longer knew what I was doing or what I was saying. I kept on saying "thank you," over and over, but that didn't seem to bother Alex.

"You're welcome, Nadia!"

"What a funny expression," I thought as I repeated

those last words. Then he waved. I left the centre, not knowing what to think of our meeting, and headed for the bus station. Alex's smile stayed with me. The next day, on the way to school with Neila, I couldn't help telling her about him. I was expecting her to tease me, or make fun of me. She turned pale instead.

"Don't tell me you're in love with a *gaouri*, Nadia! A foreigner, someone who's not one of us? Don't you understand? Your parents will kill you if they ever find out."

Her reaction surprised me. I hadn't even thought about my parents; I couldn't believe that a young man could so constantly occupy my thoughts.

"Why are you insinuating things, Neila? Who says I'm in love with him? Who told you I'm going to tell my parents about him?

She threw me a strange look. "So why are you talking about him if you're not in love with him?"

She was right. Why would I even mention him to my best friend if I weren't attracted to him?

"Let's say that I'm thinking about him, and I feel like his face is following me in my thoughts," I corrected myself.

Neila tossed her head in exasperation.

"Look, we're not talking philosophy here. By the look on your face it's clear that you're in love with him. If you're talking about him, it's because there's something in your heart."

Neila always won. I was angry with myself for having mentioned him in the first place.

"Why did you stop talking?" she snapped after a few steps in silence.

I was sulking now and didn't want to answer.

"Do you know his name?"

"Alexander."

She hesitated for a moment.

"Iskander! That's it. Call him Iskander and he'll be a Tunisian, at least in name."

I burst out laughing, and she broke into a smile at her own joke. We'd almost reached the wall and were just about to climb over it before heading to our class. From a distance we spotted Botti making his rounds. His unbuttoned jacket displayed his potbelly. Seeing him there took the wind out of our sails; we dropped the idea and made our way around the fence to enter through the main door.

Suddenly Neila said: "Looks like we're unlucky in love, you and me. I love a boy who's in prison, and you love an American, what *zhar!*"

We both laughed boisterously. Neila was my best friend, I was more certain of it with every passing day. She was absolutely right; we had no luck at all.

EIGHTEEN

Tunis, December 18, 2010

By now I'd come to know Ettadamoun Township. I'd first gone there with Donia. The streets were full of potholes and the mud stuck to our shoes, making them heavy and cumbersome. We did our best to jump over the puddles that had formed after a downpour that was like buckets of water being dumped on our heads—a frigid, stinging shower that lasted only a few minutes. This was rain and wind like I'd never seen before in Tunis. You couldn't make out a thing. I'd been helping Donia with her activities for the last several days. Our agreement was working perfectly. I was convinced I'd made the right decision, that I was getting involved in the right cause.

Things weren't always easy to understand. I was caught somewhere between black and white, between

Tunisian and Canadian. I was a hostage in a barely rec-
ognizable place I couldn't tear myself away from. Peace
and chaos existed all at once; so did past and present.
Perhaps that's why I'd found a place for myself here
and slipped into this extremely narrow, almost invisible space.

DONIA PICKED ME up for a visit to Jamel's. "Something
terrible has happened," she said, wide-eyed and tight
lipped. I made no attempt to learn more; I knew she
would tell me everything soon. Visibility was almost
zero. Several times along the way, I was sure we would
hit the vehicles ahead of us. But Donia kept calm: she
bent forward, looking straight ahead, her clenched jaw
moving continually back and forth. The windshield
wipers swept back and forth in a syncopated rhythm.

By the time we reached the township, the rain had
ended as abruptly as it began. The wind dropped and
everything returned to normal. Donia parked the car
next to a vacant lot. We could make out the metro rails
as they emerged from the soil on the curve. Plastic bags
were everywhere, and the piles of trash had been beaten
down by the rain.

"We're going to see Jamel. He lives one street over."

Donia pointed to a row of houses in the distance.
I wasn't paying close attention to what she was saying. All the dwellings looked the same: saturated with

poverty and grime, crowded close together. Sheet-metal doors were painted green, black, or blue. A few inhabitants were out front of their houses, backs bent, clearing water from their front stoops with outsize scrapers.

"What's going on? What are those people doing?" I asked with surprise.

"They're sweeping the water out of their houses. Thank God the rain stopped, otherwise there would have been flooding."

Everything in Ettadamoun Township told of poverty. I could see it on the tiny houses hunched up against one another. At the grocery store, Supermarquet le Bonheur, the bottled gas locked in a cage made the decor even sadder. A few children gathered in front of the grocery were sharing a small bottle of yogurt, passing it around. Nearby was an automotive repair shop with tires heaped outside, waiting patiently for the moment when they would be called into service to replace a blow-out. And there were rundown dwellings with peeling paint, cracks in the walls like giant scars on a face. You couldn't tell where the sidewalk began and the street ended. I hardly knew where to walk. I followed Donia in silence. We finally came to a small house all but hidden by a tall fence. A shrub that looked more like a miniature rubber tree spread its wide leaves just in front of us. My shoes were soaked, and I could feel the cold creeping through my body.

Jamel opened the gate. His face was half hidden, so I couldn't interpret his expression. Donia and I hurried inside. We crossed a small veranda where a lone tree stood upright in a patch of earth ringed with broken floor tiles and stones. Rivulets of water poured down from the gutters like tiny waterfalls. Donia seemed quite at home. The house was dark; no doors were visible, not even a hallway. I found myself in a room with two beds, each one pushed up against the wall. A few plastic chairs were scattered about, with a glowing computer on a table in the centre. Donia sat down on the edge of one of the beds. I followed suit.

Jamel spoke slowly. There were dark circles around his eyes and his hair was mussed, like a boy who'd just been awakened.

"Things are happening fast. A young man set fire to himself in Sidi Bouzid yesterday. He wanted to call attention to his situation after a policewoman slapped him and stopped him from parking his pushcart in the street."

I noticed Donia digging her fingers into the mattress. "Is he dead?"

"He's seriously burned, no one knows what will become of him," Jamel answered, dazed at the news.

"What are we going to do?" asked Donia, trying to get comfortable on the edge of the bed.

"We've got to do something."

She looked at me with questioning eyes, as though I had the answer.

"Maybe start a petition, or hold a demonstration? I remember when a property developer wanted to put up a tall building on our street, my mother and the neighbours fought back. Mom asked me and my classmates to collect signatures. I refused. At first, I thought her demands were ridiculous, and I didn't want my friends to take me for a nutcase. Those were adult matters, I thought. I finally gave in, we gathered hundreds of signatures and stopped the project. But I'm not sure the same tactic would work here. People are talking about injustice, about lives lost, about police terrorizing people."

Jamel and Donia stared at me as if I'd set off a bomb.

"Lila, you can't be serious! That's not how things work here!" Donia shot back with a frown. "Nobody would ever sign a petition. People are scared."

Sheepishly I stopped, but Jamel exclaimed: "Why not, Donia? We could do something like that, but be careful to conceal our real names. Send out a communiqué on Facebook to all our friends to let them know what's happened, and ask them to share it with their friends. Wouldn't that be great, girls?"

"Absolutely! Let's do it!"

I was startled to find myself talking again. Jamel's words gave me confidence.

"I could translate it into English. That way people in other countries would have an idea of what's going on here."

Jamel's face darkened once again.

"Fine, but we've got to be careful. We could get arrested at any time. Sami told me yesterday that all Facebook accounts and blogs were under constant surveillance by the presidential palace in Carthage. They're ready to arrest everybody. They've totally lost their bearings."

Uncle Mounir's face suddenly appeared in front of me. His face, hardened by years of injustice, was smiling. Had he been afraid of acting when he visited construction sites and spoke to the young apprentice bricklayers to mobilize them and inform them of their rights? Had he been paralyzed with fear? Of course not. He believed in what he was doing. Unfortunately, he paid a high price for his freedom. I was about ready to tell Donia and Jamel about Uncle Mounir's experience when Jamel cut me off.

"But there's already one man who's paid a high price, and he's hovering between life and death. I don't want my children to judge me for not having acted. Would you like to know what I think of fear? I hate everything about it. I've had enough of being haunted by fear, fear that's paralyzed us for years. Never again. From this day on, I'm looking you in the eyes and telling you I'm a free man!"

I broke out in goosebumps. There was no need for me to tell Uncle Mounir's story. Jamel's was enough. It was all Donia could do to hold back her tears. Now she was sitting cross-legged on the mattress. I agreed with Jamel. I dared to hope that we were on the verge of a great disturbance, only this time it would be a disturbance with a happy outcome. All of a sudden Donia broke her silence.

"But Jamel, if they find you and arrest you, we'll be behind you, we'll do everything to see you again."

Donia glanced at me and, for the first time that afternoon, I saw her smile. Jamel sat down in front of his computer. We stood up from the bed and drew two chairs over next to him.

Jamel and Donia began to draft an open letter about the young street vendor who set himself on fire and about the abject response of the authorities.

"I set up a new Facebook page named Free Tunisia. This letter will be my first post. I'll begin by providing information. But tomorrow, I'll ask people to start taking action—"

Donia interrupted him: "Such as coming out into the streets, shouting slogans, putting an end to police brutality. What do you think?"

"Now you're the one who's pushing Jamel to take the lead?" I asked her sarcastically.

"It's called solidarity! I feel like I'm sprouting wings."

Despite the tension, Jamel and I laughed out loud. Donia's enthusiasm had restored her upbeat mood. Now it was her turn to smile.

"You know something, Lila? I don't regret a thing. I'm so happy I met you. There's something about you, something I can't put my finger on. Innocence, bravado, something magical."

I blushed. No one had ever talked to me that way before.

"Thanks Donia, but let me assure you: there's nothing magical about me. We have to thank my Uncle Mounir; he's the one who inspired me. It was his courage that led me to you. I can feel his presence here among us, I swear it!"

Donia and Jamel had no idea what I was talking about. They thought I was getting carried away. The three of us were sitting there in this dark room, in a poor district of Tunis—one of the worst I'd ever seen, and far, far from whatever I'd experienced in Canada. Who would ever have thought I'd be doing what I was doing today with my new friends? Mom's hair would be standing straight up on her head. Funny—never had I felt so at ease as in that darkened room, in that impoverished house, in that township called Solidarity, one of the poorest in Tunis, thousands of miles away from Ottawa.

ΠΙΠΕΤΕΕΠ

Tunis, March 1984

MOUNIR WOULD SERVE SEVEN years in prison. Once more, we heard the news from little Mohamed. Neila no longer—almost never—mentioned his name. She wanted to forget him, she said. But I knew she was lying. Mounir was always in her thoughts. We hadn't seen Mohamed since the day he'd told us his brother had been arrested. Neila and I thought the family had moved. But one day, on our way to school we ran into him again. He had the same childish gait but this time accompanied by the look of a man grown up too fast. He was whistling, his hands in his pockets, his school bag hanging by lengths of string.

"Hey, Mohamed! What are you doing here?"

"I'm going to school, as you can see," he shot back

in a neutral, almost indifferent tone of voice.

"How's Mounir?" asked Neila who, slowly recovering from her surprise, suddenly understood what had happened.

He stopped short at the sound of his brother's name. It was as if he'd just come from far away. He looked at us long and hard.

Then he came closer and whispered with a grave face: "Mounir's still in prison. I can't go to see him. They don't let kids in. Mother visits him every Friday. I really miss him. The last time, Father told me that Mounir would be in prison seven years..."

"It's just not true! Nothing but lies," Neila interrupted him. "Who told you those lies?"

I stepped forward quickly to stop her from saying anything else.

Little Mohamed stared at Neila with startled eyes, then went on: "Me neither, I don't believe those stories. Seven years, that's too much. I'll almost be finished my *lycée* by the time he's released. I won't even recognize my own brother."

All Neila could do was stammer:

"C—, ca—, can we visit him? What's the name of the prison where they're keeping him?"

"I don't know. You'll have to ask my father. But I heard him mention the 'new prison' a couple of times."

Neila and I said nothing more. We knew the name

of the main prison in Tunis. Everyone knew it, except children like Mohamed. Neila opened her mouth to speak but thought better of it. Mohamed went off to school, with his little boy's gait.

"Don't you want to visit him?" I asked Neila, as we got underway once more.

"You can't be serious! What do you think I should show up at the prison as? His fiancée-in-waiting? His wife-to-be? Or do you think I should tell the guards like it is, that I'm his girlfriend? You want another scandal, is that it? Him being in prison isn't enough for you?"

Neila's outburst took me aback. I hadn't expected that she would react this way.

"Calm down, Neila, I didn't want to hurt your feelings. I swear I wasn't thinking any such thing. What an idiot I am! Such an idea never even occurred to me. It's true, all those considerations went way over my head."

Neila said nothing. She seemed off balance. We'd almost reached the *lycée*. All of a sudden she turned to me and said: "Nadia, I don't want to go to school any more. I feel like my head is going to explode. It's too much for me. And it's so unfair for Mounir."

Then she broke down and began to sob. I took her in my arms and tried to comfort her. Her whole body was shaking. She had never seemed so frail to me, so vulnerable. Mounir's arrest was a tragedy of an entirely different order. A tragedy that seemingly had no beginning, nor end; one that was consuming her inside.

As I hugged Neila, I noticed Sonia parking her BMW in the teachers' parking lot. She could afford to ignore the regulations. Her father worked at the Ministry of the Interior. He was the police chief; maybe he had ordered Mounir's arrest. I loathed her now even more than before. Neila remained clasped in my embrace for a few more seconds. Then, gently, she pulled free.

"I don't want to keep up my studies anymore," she said, eyes red and face wracked by emotion. "Get an education, what for? To become like the others? To perpetuate injustice?"

"How are you supposed to fight injustice, then? With ignorance, apathy, stupidity? You want to run and hide and let them get away with it? No, Neila. I don't think Mounir went to prison so that you can stop living and turn your back on reality."

She wasn't looking at me; she stared off into the distance.

"Listen carefully, Neila. Mounir is in prison. He'll be there for one year, two years, seven years. It's too much, and I know it, but one day he'll walk free. You've got to hang on, for his sake. He needs you."

Once more she looked away. We heard the bell, a jarring sound that wrenched us from our thoughts. We had to hurry. Class would begin in a few minutes. Neila looked down and walked on beside me. Resignation had overcome her. The world of injustice had won. I spotted Sonia; she was laughing boisterously along with one of the boys in the class. I gritted my teeth, but this wasn't the time to be thinking about Sonia. I knew I had to fend off whatever life threw my way; my friendship with Neila — and my own survival — demanded it.

Botti was waiting for us at the main entrance, holding open one of the doors. His whistle hung from his neck as if he were a soccer referee. He fancied himself the school police and played the role to perfection. We all lived in fear of him. But the truth was, he prepared us for the outside world. He prepared us to fear the authorities, to fear daily humiliation and abuse of power. Botti did it all, all the time. And we, the students? We were a well-trained flock of sheep that followed orders without believing them. Fear held us back. Behind his back we detested him, made fun of him, and waited for him to fall so that we could trample him and break all the rules. But we still lived in constant fear. Fear of our parents. fear for our future career, fear of confronting injustice. Mounir had made up his mind to defy fear, to change the way things were. He had attempted to challenge the regime, and now he was in prison. No friends, no comrades could visit him. There, among the rats and the cockroaches, he was languishing alongside others like him, who had also dared. As for us, we were on the other side. The side of fear. Feigning ignorance or actually being ignorant of what was going on around us. Powerless. Neila and I had no idea of how to carry on with the job Mounir had started.

"Come on, girls, get moving! I'm closing the doors. Hurry up; class is starting. What's going on here anyway? Is everybody late today?"

I didn't even want to look at him. He disgusted me. The fingers that held the door open were repugnant. Other students were crushing their cigarette butts not far from the door, then pushing past us. The smell of cigarette smoke mixed with sweat was overwhelming. Botti was getting impatient.

Neila and I hurried through the doorway. Botti pulled back his fat, cigar-shaped fingers and the door slammed behind him. We made straight for our classroom. The instructor hadn't yet arrived; the students were waiting inside. All hell was breaking loose. Two boys had left their seats and were kicking a plastic ball back and forth at the rear of the room. Sonia, true to form, was waiting in her usual place, right in front of the instructor's desk. She'd pulled out a mirror and was arranging her hair. I didn't even dare to look at her. Her naked ambition and egotism were so obvious. She was responsible for all our troubles. It was true! Her happiness had robbed us of Mounir. In her face I saw all the injustice that surrounded us. Inside, I was seething.

The more I looked at her, the more her indifference twisted my guts.

As I passed her desk on my way to my usual place, I couldn't stop myself from hissing: "Primping for Monsieur Kamel, eh? Well, you're nothing! A big, fat stinking zero. That's what you are!"

Neila jabbed me with her elbow. "Shhh!"

Sonia dropped her mirror. Her mascara-lined eyes stared at me as though I were a ghost. She got to her feet and arched her back like a cat ready to pounce.

"Watch your mouth, you little slut! Mind your own hand-me-downs and the little char girls that follow you around. You can keep your advice to yourself."

I have to admit that I'd underestimated Sonia's ability to react. I wanted to play with the big girls, but she was more ready for a fight than me. I didn't know how to respond. But I was proud to have knocked her off her pedestal. I was trying to think up a comeback, but Neila nudged me hard with her elbow. A deathly silence settled over the classroom. Everybody had heard the exchange; even the two boys who'd been playing ball had sat down, anxious to watch the confrontation. We had become the centre of attention.

"The instructor's coming, will you please shut up now," Neila whispered in my ear.

But there was no holding me back. I was going to go after Sonia, after the privilege that she flaunted so insolently, after her success-at-any-price behaviour, using all her charm and her father's influence.

"If you're so sure, why don't you tell everybody that you're a little numbskull, and that the only way you can get a passing mark is by seducing Monsieur Kamel, that poor bugger. Come on, you big fat idiot, tell us!"

I'd gotten my revenge. I'd shut that conceited little bitch up. I had more to say, but Neila clapped her hand over my mouth. I turned around to stop her, and it was at that moment that I saw Monsieur Kamel placing his black briefcase atop his desk. His eyes were boring into me. He'd heard it all, seen it all. My accusing words resounded in the classroom in a joyful noise. The whole class was waiting for the other shoe to drop. Neila had slumped onto the desk next to mine. Despair flooded over her face. I didn't move.

Sonia was weeping loudly.

"Did you hear, sir, what that little vermin said?" asked Sonia. "I can't imagine anyone could be so low. Oh my God, how rude is she!"

An offended look on her face, Sonia swung her head from right to left. Then she delicately wiped the mascara that was running down her cheeks.

"Mademoiselle Mabrouk, take your things and leave. I have no need of students like you in my class. I will prepare a report on your unseemly behaviour."

I picked up my schoolbag. Neila had turned pale.

She stared at me with beseeching eyes. "Go say you're sorry! Go on, do it now!" she begged.

I made as if I'd heard nothing. For the first time in my life I felt strong and confident. I had just spoken the truth, the truth that everyone knew but pretended not to see. It was none of my business. Fine. But I wanted to hit back, for Mounir, for Neila. I was the feminine version of Étienne Lantier, after all. The blood was boiling in my veins. I was a heroine now, but I wouldn't be much longer. I would pay dearly for my insolence. Before long I would be brought back into line. For in this country, you couldn't live without keeping in line.

TWENTY

Tunis, December 28, 2010

THAT EVENING, AFTER A long day spent with Donia
and Jamel writing short pieces, posting them on
Facebook, and answering questions online, I returned to an apartment seemingly locked in silence.
Aunt Neila and Uncle Mounir must have gone out,
I thought, perhaps visiting friends on the next floor
down. They'd done the same thing a few weeks ago.
But after closing the door, I heard the sound of voices
from the living room and noticed a dim light. There
they were, seated side by side in front of the TV,
watching the news in silence. As quietly as I could,
I sat down beside them. I felt at home. I was part of
the family now, after all, and no longer the foreign
girl trying to find herself. Aunt Neila smiled at me

without a word, and Uncle Mounir gestured with his head as if to tell me that he'd seen me and to greet me. I responded with a smile and a nod.

On the screen, President Zine El Abidine Ben Ali was in a hospital room surrounded by doctors and nurses. The person on the bed was wrapped from head to toe in white bandages: a living mummy. The president stood at a distance, a worried look on his face, listening to the group of physicians that accompanied him.

"What a hypocrite!" Uncle Mounir burst out. "What's he doing at the bedside of someone the regime's stooges drove to suicide? What a pathetic farce!"

It didn't take me long to realize that the sick man was Mohamed Bouazizi, the same man whose story Donia, Jamel, and I were following. The man who set himself afire to preserve what was left of his dignity.

Aunt Neila was wiping her eyes as she wept silently.

"To ask the people for forgiveness, perhaps?" I suggested calmly.

Uncle Mounir smiled at me. "For sure, but this time it won't work. It isn't the same people as twenty-five years ago. The regime's days are numbered. I can feel it. Some of my friends at the UGTT told me that demonstrations are being organized all over the country, that it's just beginning."

I saw Aunt Neila turn pale. She hadn't yet spoken. She sighed and then spoke: "That's what you're hoping, but it's not sure that people are ready to bring down the wall of fear."

"Neila, don't be pessimistic, I beg you. Things have changed. It's not like in our day. Can't you see that even Lila, who's from Canada, is involved with what's happening here? And her friends are, too." Uncle Mounir's gaze was grave, and focused directly on me.

"I don't know what things were like in your day," I said. "But judging by the comments we're getting on Jamel's blog, and if I can trust what Donia and Jamel have been telling me over the last few days, it's clear that everybody wants a change. I don't know if it will happen. The police are still monitoring everything. The Internet isn't free. Jamel writes his articles using a pseudonym. They could throw him in jail at any moment."

Aunt Neila seemed to have found her argument. "You see, Mounir, it isn't as simple as you think. Ben Ali controls everything: the Internet, the police, the people. Watch what you're doing, Lila. Your friends Donia and Jamel seem sincere, but if they were ever arrested and—may God protect you!—anything were to happen to you, what would we do then? Did you ever think of the consequences? And your mother, what about her? Nadia would never forgive me."

Her mention of Mom's name made me cringe. I hadn't said a word to my mother about anything. The fears she expressed a few days before were turning out to be well-founded. If she knew what I was up to, she'd die of fear.

"Please, don't say a word to her! She'd be frightened for nothing. I know my mom. She sent me to learn Arabic. For me to get involved in a mass uprising is the last thing she'd expect..."

Aunt Neila's features hardened. Uncle Mounir switched off the TV and went off into the kitchen. I could hear the tinkling of glasses, and I thought he was making tea. From the kitchen he called out: "Leave her be, Neila, don't try to frighten her. She knows her way around, plus she's a Canadian, the cops—pigs, the whole lot of them!—can't touch her. They're too cowardly to touch a foreigner."

Aunt Neila was getting more upset by the minute.

"But can't you see that Nadia entrusted her daughter to us? We've got to take care of her. I don't feel good about this situation. If things get out of hand, it'll be too late. I'm telling you, I don't feel good about it at all. I don't want to have to lie to her."

I could understand Aunt Neila. She was thinking back to Uncle Mounir's arrest; she didn't want the same thing to happen to her best friend's daughter.

"Things have changed a lot. We're very careful. We're using the Internet to get the news out there because young people feel like there's no place for them.

We're in touch with all the other young people in the country. I think it's fantastic. You should be happy!"

Uncle Mounir came back into the living room carrying a tray with three steaming saucers filled with a greyish-green mixture. I screwed up my mouth.

"Its *drôo*, what you call sorghum," he said. "It's like a pudding. We make it with milk, sugar, and sorghum flour. It's a winter dish. Here, grab a spoon and take a bite. It's delicious, you'll see. It'll warm you up."

Aunt Neila was so upset by our argument that she didn't even touch her pudding. Meanwhile, Uncle Mounir was doing everything he could to calm us down. I slid a spoonful of this curious cream into my mouth. It had an interesting taste; I took another spoonful. By then I had the feeling that I couldn't stop. The pudding was warm, comforting.

Aunt Neila was looking at me with a mother's sweetness, as if she'd forgotten that only a couple of minutes before she was in complete disagreement with my idea of telling Mom nothing about my new activities with Donia and Jamel.

"What if you sent your mother a message telling her what you're doing, without too many details? Don't you think it would be better for everybody? How about it, Lila? What do you think?"

I didn't want to answer, first because I was too caught up in eating my tasty *drôo*, but also because I wasn't sure it would be the right tactic. A simple message wouldn't be enough. Mom would want more details; she wouldn't be satisfied with a few vague and empty sentences.

"She'd never understand what I'm doing. A message like that would frighten her. She'd panic, I know it."

Uncle Mounir threw a reproachful glance at Aunt Neila.

"Enough with the negative ideas, Neila. Everything will be fine. Like I said, Lila is a big girl now—"

I interrupted impatiently: "After all, I've got less than two weeks left before I go back to Canada. I don't think there'll be any huge changes between now and then."

A look of sadness settled over her face. Already my upcoming departure had begun to affect her.

"It's true. You're probably right."

She didn't seem all that convinced, but she didn't say anything else. She leaned over the tray and handed me a second saucer.

"Have another. Looks like you're taking to *drôo*. I'll make you some every day if you like."

I took the saucer and began eating eagerly. Mouth full and tongue burning, I asked her: "Don't you like it? It's really delicious. I never tasted anything like it before, like toasted almonds."

Once more, a shadow passed over her face, then she smiled a sad smile.

"I had too much when I was a little girl. Mother, may God bless her soul, prepared it for me on winter mornings. My father..." She fell silent, then resumed: "He made us eat it all winter long. But I couldn't stand the taste — it made me sick to my stomach. I'd fill my mouth with *drôo*, then leave the table and go spit it out in the toilet."

She shivered, and I decided it would be best not to ask her any more questions.

Uncle Mounir smiled.

"Look how delicate your Aunt Neila is, Lila. She eats only the finest foods: Swiss chocolate, buttery crois-sants, candied orange peel, and such. At our place, we ate everything, even mouldy bread. Same as we fed the animals. No difference. We didn't have a choice — we had to live."

I realized from Uncle Mounir's sarcastic tone that he wanted to tease his wife. And now, she was smiling.

"Yes, that's it, you play the victim, as though my parents were rich people."

"Compared to mine, they certainly were!"

"Fine, I'll grant you that, but I'm not quite as delicate as you claim. I'm no princess. The taste of *drôo* brings back bad memories, why don't we leave it at that?"

Then she turned to me.

"One day, when you ask your mother to tell you about me, you'll learn the truth. Uncle Mounir's got it in for me this evening. I'm not going to say anything more..."

I finished my second saucer.

"For sure, I'll ask her to tell me everything."

Uncle Mounir picked up the tray and went off to the kitchen. The evening was ending. The atmosphere had turned melancholy. I said goodnight and retired to my room.

Donia sent me an SMS: *Come by tomorrow at 10, the party's starting!*

What did she mean by "the party's starting?" What if Aunt Neila was right; what if I should talk it over with Mom? I wasn't sure about anything. No sooner had I put on my pajamas than I fell into a troubled sleep. A sleep populated with men in face masks, and police chasing them. I found myself swimming in a pool filled with *drôo*. The viscous liquid was dragging me under; I had to thrash around in order to keep afloat, while Aunt Neila and Uncle Mounir looked on silently from a distance.

TWENTY-ONE

Tunis, April, 1984

THEY EXPELLED ME FROM the *lycée*. The decision was
final. I would never attend a single class there again.
All because of my rudeness and the way I'd so terribly
insulted a member of the teaching staff. The news
hit me like a thunderclap directly above my head.
Monsieur Kamel had reported the way I'd insulted
Sonia. Immediately after that, my case had come before the school's disciplinary board. "The board of farce
and injustice" is what it really was. I could not defend
myself. Overnight, people turned their backs on me as
if I had a contagious disease. I was the girl everybody
was pointing at because of the terrible false accusations
I'd made against my instructor. Those were things that
could not be spoken aloud as I had done, but that people

whispered in the hallways, and behind the backs of the instructors and the monitors.

Still, everybody knew very well that Sonia was using her charms to wrap Monsieur Kamel around her finger and improve her grades. Everybody knew that he liked her infantile and dangerous games. But nobody would say a word. All the students wanted to do was to succeed, to go on to university. Everybody understood what you had to do in this country. Everybody but me. I wanted to play the heroine. I wanted to struggle against injustice. I wanted to avenge Mounir. And I'd failed. All the members of the board sided with Monsieur Kamel and against the pariah I'd become: a frivolous, spoiled brat. The parents' representative on the board, who was also a member of the Destourian Party cell in our district, stated that I was a "microbe" and that I had "endangered the other students" and for that reason alone, I needed to be "eradicated." My father told me the whole story. He had gone to the board meeting and done his best to defend me, the poor man. All for naught. He praised my good grades, my faultless academic record. It had been a youthful error, he said. I'd spoken up without knowing what I was saying; the board should pardon my bad behaviour and give me another chance.

But Father's words had simply evaporated without a trace. The decision had already been made; all that remained were the formalities. Nadia Mabrouk was an easy target. Father: civil servant with no political affiliation (doubtful case). Mother: housewife (even more doubtful). I was up against two powerful enemies: Monsieur Kamel, professor of Arabic for twenty years, and head of a family, married, a citizen beyond reproach. The second obstacle was even more formidable: Sonia Cherif. Father: Director of the Tunis police and member of the Central Committee of the Destourian Party. Mother: homemaker, French national permanently domiciled in Tunis following her marriage to a Tunisian. The game was over before it started. I should never have ventured into the enemy camp. It was too late. I'd lost. Now I would serve time in the prison of my family.

When she heard the news, Mother almost had a heart attack. She nearly died. She who'd always believed that when I won my baccalaureate, it would boost our status in the neighbourhood. She had already begun planning the little party she would throw to celebrate my graduation. Everyone knew I was a good student, and that I would succeed without any problems. But the couscous revolt had transformed me, had made me a new person. No one had seen the change coming. Suddenly I was the school dunce. Expelled. A *zoufri* in a skirt! The shame of the neighbourhood.

Father kept silent. But Mother, between bouts of

lamentation, cries of rage and pain from her heart-attack symptoms, kept on repeating: "But what got into you? Are you crazy or what? Why did you curse out that girl Sonia? Why didn't you just mind your own business, eh? You go to school to study, and you come straight home. That's all. Just like everybody else! Why aren't you like everybody else? Why?"

"Because it's the truth. I told the truth! Everybody knows it's the truth, but nobody dares to say it."

Mother let out a curse. She got up from the arm-chair she'd slumped into a couple of minutes before. She would have liked to grab me by the hair. Hit me. She'd never struck me before, but on that day, it was different. I'd destroyed her dreams. Now it was time for her to put my rebellion to an end.

Father, who seemed to be in another world, suddenly reached out and caught her arm.

"Nadia is eighteen. She's a grown-up young woman, you can't hit her."

"So that's it? There's your education for you! You've always spoiled her and now look at her! Kicked out of the *lycée* just a few months before she graduates. Now what will become of her? Secretary? Cleaning lady? Even for those miserable jobs you need a baccalaure-ate these days."

Mother was exaggerating and I knew it. My Auntie Rafika's cleaning lady only finished primary school.

She could read, and write letters to her cousin in the village. I knew because I helped her write those letters. She wrote them in *Darija*, the Arabic dialect that everybody spoke, and not the classical Arabic we studied at school, but it was better than nothing. She could read the local news in the newspapers that ran rape and robbery stories. She would tell me all about them each time we visited my aunt, and she was busy hanging the laundry on the veranda, singing the same old ballad of the two lovers meeting at night by the well.

But I didn't want to become a cleaning lady or a secretary. I knew I could continue with my studies. In fact, I was determined to.

As if Father had read my thoughts, he said to Mother: "Tomorrow, I'm going to visit a private school called *La Réussite*. I know the headmistress's husband. He's an old friend. We grew up on the same street, played ball together in the back alleys. I'll ask him if his wife will accept Nadia into her school. It's a long shot. The school year ends in two months. I don't know if she'll be accepted. But I'll try—"

"So now you're going to pay to get Nadia into a private school?" Mother interrupted. "After all, she brought it on herself. She makes the mistakes and we pay for them, is that it?"

I wept for joy. Father would save me. I didn't want to hear Mother's harsh words any more. And in any case, she was never satisfied. But I would show them that I could succeed, that my expulsion was the worst injustice in the world, and that my revolt had a positive outcome: to humiliate Sonia, the daughter of the Tunis police director. The person who had ordered Mounir's arrest.

I thought back to Neila. What would become of her without me? We would be separated. She was the one who didn't want to keep up her studies, after all. How would she manage two separations at the same time: from Mounir and now from me?

TWENTY-TWO

Tunis, December 29, 2010

TUNIS WAS HOLDING ITS breath. The revolt was heading straight for the capital at full speed. I could feel it in the air and see it in peoples' eyes. Demonstrations were breaking out in the poor districts, Donia told me. We should be getting ready to take to the streets. Mom was right, after all—or rather, her sources were more reliable than ours, here, on the ground. The Internet wasn't filtered in Canada. It was another story altogether here. In the newspapers, on radio and television, it was always the same old messages: "Our president is the greatest," "Our country is experiencing great economic success," "Tunisia is a rampart against fundamentalism and obscurantism."

I wasn't making anything up. Uncle Mounir con-

firmed it this morning. We were in the kitchen. The
radio was on. I could hear the nasal voice of the president, speaking with the intonations of a robot.

"What did he say?" I asked, curious. "I can't catch
everything."

"It's a replay of his speech yesterday. We missed it
on TV. He says violence won't be tolerated, and that
the law will be applied firmly to anyone who uses —"

"What about police brutality, about the people who
are attacking the demonstrators?"

Uncle Mounir smiled a sad smile.

"Not a word. He couldn't care less. He was a cop
before he became president."

I kept quiet. Just a few weeks ago, that tone of voice
and those words would not have meant a thing. But it
was different now. It was as if I belonged a little more
to this country, to its people. I couldn't tell whether I'd
adopted Tunisia or whether the country had adopted
me. One thing was certain: it was time to act.

"They're predicting demonstrations downtown.
Are you going to go?"

I wanted to see his reaction. He switched off the
radio. He was standing in front of the range, reaching
for the *zézoua*. The sound of coffee coming to a boil
was the signal to lift the little pot from the burner. The
Turkish coffee was ready. Its odour wafted through the
kitchen. Uncle Mounir had still not answered.

I asked him again, in a soft voice, "Are you going to go to the demonstration today?"

"What demonstration?" he replied, as if suddenly brought back to earth.

"Donia told me there will be a monster gathering of workers and trade unionists in front of UGTT headquarters, the one you told me about the other day. I don't remember the exact name of the place."

Uncle Mounir's face lit up.

"Of course! It's Mohamed Ali Square. How well I know it! It's named after Mohamed Ali El Hammi, a great nineteenth-century labour organizer who's considered the father of Tunisian trade unionism, and it's always been the symbol of the workers' cause. He's one of my heroes."

Uncle Mounir's enthusiasm seemed to overflow as he described the life and struggle of a man I'd never heard of before.

"We can go together. I'll ask Neila. Maybe she'd like to come along too. It might stir up some old memories. Who knows? She might even do something she couldn't when she was young."

Aunt Neila had just come into the kitchen on silent feet. Her eyes were puffy, as though she'd slept badly.

"Go where?" she asked, without much conviction.

"Mohamed Ali Square. There's going to be a huge dem—"

She cut him off. Her face turned white. "You can't be serious, Mounir. What about the police? And if things turn nasty, do you think it'll be kids' games? It might be risky for Lila! No, you shouldn't go!"

Uncle Mounir winked at me, as if to say that Aunt Neila was exaggerating, that she was overdoing the fear, that I shouldn't pay too much attention.

Silently I observed the couple. Two people who loved each other, two people who saw life differently. He was the kind of man who rushed ahead without thinking about the consequences, while she was cautious, wary of anything and everything. Each of them stood firm on their convictions. Even after years of separation and suffering, their souls had not changed.

I said nothing, not wanting to start a fight. I finished my glass of milk in silence. My phone began to vibrate in my pocket. I checked: it was Donia.

I'll be waiting for you at my place in fifteen minutes.

"I'm going to Donia's," I said, trying to mask my emotions.

Uncle Mounir said nothing.

Not so for Aunt Neila: "Be careful, call me, and above all, don't go near Mohamed Ali Square. It's full of *zoufris*, of people from the unions. It's no place for a young girl. You listen to me, Lila. I know what I'm talking about. Don't go, alright?"

She was all but begging. But my mind was made up.

It was clear Aunt Neila was being overprotective, even though I could understand her better now. Mom trusted her, and she didn't want anything to happen to me.

What could possibly happen, though?

I was bursting with energy and confidence, ready to take on the world. The disturbances were coming like winds of change. It wasn't time for me to start backing down.

Donia was waiting for me in front of her house, checking her cellphone. When she saw me coming, she smiled, stretched out her arms and said: "I promised to meet Jamel downtown. He'll be taking photos, and I'm going to write an article to post on Facebook. You're coming with us, right?"

I was still hesitant. Aunt Neila's voice was still ringing in my ears. Donia looked me in the eye.

"Listen, Lila, no one's forcing you to say yes. But the last time we met, at Jamel's, I had the feeling we understood each other. Whatever you make up your mind to do, you'll always be welcome."

What if we're arrested? And what if it really is a dangerous place, swarming with *zoufris*, those low-lifes who harass girls and snatch purses? Aunt Neila's words wouldn't stop running through my head. And Mom, what would she do if she knew I was participating in demonstrations? Donia sensed my apprehension.

"Sure it's dangerous, and I know it. But remember,

we discussed it all with Jamel. We're ready for a change, isn't that right? Nothing can stop us!"

She threw me a defiant look. That old fox Am Mokhtar was pacing back and forth in front of his cybercafé. The morning breeze had ruffled the few strands of hair he combed across his glistening bald patch. I couldn't have cared less. My doubts had vanished. Optimism had won the day. The winds of enthusiasm that were carrying me along swept Aunt Neila's words of caution away.

"You're right, nothing can stop us. I'm ready for anything. We're in this together."

Donia let out a cry of delight that made Am Mokhtar jump right as he was about to sit down in his plastic chair.

"Is everything okay, *binti* Donia?" he asked deviously.

"Just fine, Am Mokhtar," she shot back without even looking at him.

"I wish you a morning full of joy and jasmine, my little one," he answered, opening his newspaper and pretending to read.

Am Mokhtar's prayers were not answered. There was neither joy nor jasmine that day. Donia left her car in a parking lot, and we walked. I had no idea where I was going, and I followed Donia unquestioningly. I didn't recognize a single one of the streets or alleys that we crossed, one after another. Around us flowed a procession of people, of cars, of shops and cafés. I felt lost in the onrush of strange faces and places. After a good fifteen minutes we reached the famous square, surrounded by colonial-era buildings. The French doors and balconies were painted sky blue, faded now to a weather-worn grey. A few red flags with the star and crescent in the centre were fluttering in the wind. The shops at street level had lowered their metal shutters, but their signs were still visible. I recognized one of them: *Tunisiana*, where I bought my phone cards. Aunt Neila was right. In front of us was a shifting, rising, and falling tide of men. They all looked alike to me: black mustaches, blue jeans, leather jackets. Here and there was a head wearing a woollen cap, a grey beret, or a red *chéchia*. People were pushing and shoving. Cardboard picket signs began to appear. I couldn't read a word; my Arabic was not equal to the task. Then Jamel popped up, seemingly out of nowhere. Face gleaming with pride, he held his phone in one hand as he filmed the moving crowd.

"You showed a lot of courage, girls! We're making history, I just know it! I'm going to record everything and broadcast it online. People all around the world must see the brutality of the regime for themselves, and the dignity of our people."

Donia's eyes were gleaming with admiration. She threw her arm around his neck and kissed him on the cheek.

Jamel kept on filming unbothered. The crowd was growing larger, and I could feel a sense of acute discomfort creeping over me. What was I doing here, in this demonstration? Was it true, what Aunt Neila said, that I shouldn't have come in the first place? Then the slogans the crowd was chanting drove my anxiety away. The voices mingled then winged their way skyward as if they would reach all the way to infinity. A few people were standing on the balconies, looking dazed as they watched the crowd suddenly get underway. People marched slowly at first, then faster and faster. Donia was holding my hand. I could feel her close to me. The revolution was bringing us together. Her shoulder rubbed against mine. She repeated the chant: *"Tounous horra horra . . . wanidham ala barra."*

All of a sudden, the same words were coming out of my mouth, even though I didn't really understand them. Solidarity had caught hold of me. No more fear, no more holding back. My whole body was vibrating to the rhythm of the chanting: *"Yasqot hazb el destour, yasqot jallad ech'ab!"* As if it were an incomprehensible prayer, I repeated the words. The heat generated by the crowd seemed to have stuck our sweating hands together. Jamel had disappeared, swept away by the wave.

Then the crowd came to an abrupt halt. Police in

riot gear protected by their shields were blocking the street. Behind them was another group of demonstrators, people who still supported the regime.

The roaring of the crowd ceased. Tensions were rising. You could have heard a pin drop. The vanguard of the demonstration wanted to push forward, but the police were blocking the way, helmets on their heads, riot clubs in their hands. I could hear the heavy breathing of the demonstrators around me. Donia looked me in the eye.

"They want to disperse us. Whatever happens, follow me. We have to stick together, okay?"

I nodded. Things were turning ugly. Shouting broke out again. Cursing. The crowd backed up.

"What's going on, Donia?"

"No idea. They won't let us move forward."

The shouting was louder now.

"The police are beating the demonstr—"

Donia didn't have time to finish. An irresistible force, another wave, was pushing us in the opposite direction, pushing back against us. Against my will, I found myself walking backward. My hand released Donia's. The human tide carried me along. I could recognize the national anthem; its words were humming all about me: *"Ihda chaabou wayman arada el hayyat, fala bouda an yastajiba al qadar."*

I recognized those words! Mom would sing them

when she was in a festive mood or feeling homesick. I never learned them, but now, separated from my friends, heart pounding, hemmed in by the bodies that surrounded me on all sides, I could feel them coming back to me. Joy swept over me. Life had taken on new meaning.

Someone — or something — struck me. I doubled over, ribs aching with pain.

"*Horyaa, karama, watanyaa...*" The words kept coming. I could barely stand straight. "*Horyaa...*"

What did it mean? No one was there to tell me. Not Donia. Not Jamel. My friends were gone. Swallowed up by the crowd. Pulled forward by the call to freedom. Pain swept over me. I couldn't walk. I stumbled. I felt myself falling.

TWENTY-THREE

Tunis, April, 1984

NOTHING WORKED. FATHER DID not manage to enrol me at *La Réussite*, the private *lycée*. The school's director wouldn't accept me. What school would accept a student only a few months before the end of the school year?

"You can always try next year. There's a strong likelihood that we will accept her," she told him.

But that wasn't the real reason for her refusal. Neila had told me the night before, when she'd come over to bring me her class notes so that I could keep up with my courses.

"Nadia, did you know that Monsieur Kamel's wife is a French instructor at *La Réussite*?"

The information hit me like a powerful wave. My limbs began to quiver.

"How do you know?"

"I found out by accident. I overheard some of the girls in our class talking. They were saying that Monsieur Kamel is married to a French teacher who works at *La Réussite*, the private *lycée*."

"Do you really think the director would have admitted me knowing that I insulted the husband of one of their teachers?"

Neila fell silent. That was her way of answering my question. Tears filled her eyes.

"Look what's happened to us! First they throw Mounir in prison, and now they kick you out of school. And it's all because of that damned couscous revolt! If things had only stayed the same, if people hadn't come out into the streets to demonstrate, if Mounir hadn't wanted to become a Tunisian Étienne Lantier, if only he'd kept his mouth shut. None of this would ever have happened."

She was weeping now; tears flowed down her cheeks and her shoulders were heaving. I began to cry as well. I couldn't hold myself back.

"But Mounir did it for a good cause. He's in prison, but he educated other young people who have come forward to denounce corruption, who know their rights better and won't let a handful push them around. Isn't that something wonderful? So I lost my school year! What's one year in someone's life? I exposed Sonia, who was cozying up to the teacher to get good marks. I showed her up and I don't regret it. Don't you appreciate what we managed to do?"

Neila smiled bitterly. She was far from convinced. My words had done little to comfort her.

"You're saying that to make yourself feel better. But you know very well, deep down, that it's the poor and the underprivileged that paid the highest price, and are still paying. You humiliated Sonia, that's true. But she couldn't care less. You know very well that the only thing that matters to her is herself. She'll graduate and succeed, and you know it as well as I do."

Neila was right. We'd lost everything. Were we so naive when we tried to play the hero?

"But Alex is twenty-three, the same age as Mounir, and he left home to work abroad. He wants to change the world, too. That's the reason he came to Tunisia. He wanted to find out about other countries, about other people. Learn from other cultures."

Neila stopped crying. She wiped her eyes with the back of her hand. The crisis was over. In her eyes I could see curiosity mingled with sadness.

"And you're comparing our lives with the life of an American?"

"Not American, Neila. Canadian."

She waved her hand as though brushing away a fly.

"As far as I'm concerned, they're all the same. What's

the difference? A Canadian's dreams aren't the same as a Tunisian's. *Kif-kif* it's not, sweetie. Canada is a rich country. Here, we live in poverty. We don't have a clue what democracy means. Here, we're knee deep in shit. And that's the truth. That Alex of yours doesn't have to fear for his life. In fact, he's having the time of his life, and dreaming his bourgeois dreams at the same time." Now Neila's lips were trembling.

"What's made you so cynical? Why don't you want to believe in what Mounir was fighting for? Why do you want to ignore the dreams of the young people? Our dreams, Neila?" As I spoke I lowered my voice. I didn't want Mother to hear. Ever since they'd expelled me, she watched my every move and made my life miserable. The expression on Neila's face softened.

"I just got carried away, that's all! And what does Alex have to do with what we're talking about anyway?"

I smiled and lowered my voice further still: "Maybe he'll help me out of the fix I'm in. Maybe I can go to Canada."

Neila froze. "Are you crazy? Tell me you're crazy! I can't believe you're saying this!"

"I've still got my head on my shoulders!" I took her hands in mine and whispered: "It's the only way out for me. If I have nothing to hope for here, then I'll leave." I hastened to add, "I'll leave along with Alex."

Neila shut her eyes. I could hear her regular breathing. Something bonded us together: Nadia and Neila for life. Alex had changed everything. The couscous revolt had transformed me. Separation was coming at high speed. I didn't know what had come over me. I had promised myself I wouldn't tell a soul I was thinking of leaving, with Alex. But Neila's words had cleared the way.

After they expelled me from the *lycée*, I went almost every day to the cultural centre. One day, Alex asked me if I would go with him to visit the Zitouna Mosque, in the heart of the *medina*. It was only a short walk from the centre. Without a moment's hesitation I accepted.

It was a fine day. Alex told me about the books he loved. I told him about my life, describing the incident with Monsieur Kamel. He heard me out, up until the very end, and said nothing. I felt at peace with him. The *souk* was deserted. There were no tourists. The craftsmen were in their shops. Here and there, some men were drinking tea and listening to the radio. An unusual calm had settled over the city.

"What are you going to do now?" he asked.

"I don't know. I'll live at home. Maybe I can register in a computer school so I can learn to type on a keyboard."

He looked at me with wary eyes.

"No, don't do that. Follow your passion. Study

English. You have to finish your studies."

"My father is trying to register me for the coming year. Maybe it will work, but if not . . ."

"If not, what? Listen to me! I've got a proposal to make. I'm serious. I can help you study in Canada."

We'd reached the entrance to the great Zitouna Mosque. Rays of light shone delicately from the stone columns. The arcades, arched to provide protection from the sun, revealed the brown wooden beams of the ceiling in perfect alignment. Dried fruit sellers, oblivious to the age-old stones that watched over them and their merchandise, sang the praises of the walnuts, hazelnuts, sugared almonds, and candies that filled their stalls and their shelves.

I couldn't believe my ears.

"Me? Go to Canada?"

"Why not?" he replied with that simultaneously serious and sympathetic expression of his.

"And my parents? I'm supposed to leave them behind, just like that?"

"You'll talk to them."

We were climbing up the stairs that led to the main gate of the mosque. Alex pulled a camera from his backpack. *Click, click*: he was taking photos.

"Stop that immediately!"

A voice ordered him to put away the camera. A powerfully built man with black eyes was giving us the once-over. He turned to me, almost shouting. His words stopped me in my tracks.

"Tell the gentleman he cannot enter the mosque. It's forbidden for the *kuffar*," he said, disdainfully.

I turned to Alex. He'd already understood. With a broad smile he said: "I know. No need to explain. I'm not allowed to enter."

Blushing with emotion, embarrassed by the guard's rudeness, and still stunned by Alex's offer, I couldn't utter a word.

"I'll come back another time to take photos. When you're with a group of tourists they're less rude."

We turned back. Alex lived in an apartment in Salammbô, a Tunis suburb. Every day he took the TGM train, the Tunis-La Goulette-La Marsa, to come to work, then walked a good twenty minutes along Avenue Bourguiba until he reached the American cultural centre.

By this time, the shops were all closed. Our footsteps echoed on the broad irregular paving stones that formed the road surface of the *souk*, which dated back to Ottoman times.

"Are you angry?" asked Alex. "I shouldn't have asked you to come to Canada."

"No, no! I'm not angry. The problem is, my parents will never let me leave for Canada all alone. It's hard for a girl from here to travel abroad, especially someone in my situation. I don't have a diploma, no scholarship, nothing."

He fell silent. Already I regretted my words. I felt as if I was looking for pity.

I tried another approach: "Maybe my father would accept the idea, but Mother, never!"

"Funny, I'd have thought exactly the opposite. Why your mother and not your father?"

"Because Father is much more liberal. He studied for a few years in France. For Mother, it's tradition that counts. That's all that matters for her."

He startled me by asking: "And you, are you traditional like your mother or liberal like your father?"

We'd reached the bus stop. The *souk* had disappeared behind us. This was where I would catch my bus to go home. I hesitated a moment, then said: "I don't know. I'm still trying to find out."

He looked me in the eye. A penetrating look. I felt my heart palpitating like the time when I saw a man and a woman kiss for the first time on television, before Mother could start sighing and Father shut off the set. I wanted to take Alex's hand, but I was shaking so much that it was all I could do to tell him: "Good evening, Alex, and thanks for the lovely walk."

He walked off without a word, striding calmly and confidently. A few moments later, after I'd taken a seat in the bus, I saw him walking along Avenue Bourguiba. How much I wanted to walk by his side!

TWENTY-FOUR

Tunis, January 3, 2011

UNCLE MOUNIR SAVED MY life. I didn't even know it
was him at the time. The blood was pounding in my
temples. I couldn't see straight; I was about to black out.
The pain in my back was unbearable. His hand gripped
my arm, the same powerful arm with the long scar. He
had also come out to demonstrate alongside his former
trade union comrades. Luckily, he caught sight of me in
the crowd and came to my rescue. I'd taken a blow to
the back. Someone had shoved me; I couldn't breathe.
Uncle Mounir was only a few paces away. Was it coincidence? I had no idea. Maybe he'd been watching over
me from a distance. Later he said it was pure chance;
he didn't even know I was there. Nothing was broken.
It was a brutal blow combined with a panic attack. That

was what the doctor said. I was a bit claustrophobic. When Aunt Neila saw me walk in the door, my face ashen, eyes haggard, and clothing dishevelled, she came close to giving her husband a tongue-lashing.

"So, you took her along with your pals, isn't that it? You almost got her killed!"

I didn't have the strength to interrupt. I shook my head "no" but it did no good. Aunt Neila was in attack mode.

Uncle Mounir defended himself like a little boy being scolded by an overprotective mother: "She went on her own, with her friends. I met her on Mohamed Ali Square. The police attacked. It was all downhill from there."

Aunt Neila calmed down a bit. She turned to me: "Lila, I told you it was dangerous. I told you the police aren't choirboys. I know what I'm talking about. I lived through those seven years when Mounir was in jail—those years were hell. Have you forgotten, Mounir, how the police treated you when they arrested you? Have you forgotten how the plainclothes police followed you everywhere after you were released, like two watch-dogs who never left you in peace? What's the matter with you? How can you pretend everything is normal? Why won't anybody listen to me?"

I'd never heard Aunt Neila rant like that. She was normally so gentle, so motherly, so loving, but what had happened to me had transformed her into a raging storm. She had never spoken about her husband's arrest so openly in front of me. Uncle Mounir, his face still showing the stress of the day's events, helped me lie down on the sofa in the living room, and then went over to sit down close to Aunt Neila.

"There, there my dearest. It's nothing. Lila is safe and sound. It could have been worse, I admit it. But thank God, nothing too serious happened. Neila, listen to me: I haven't forgotten a thing, and you can be sure that it's because I haven't forgotten the way they arrested me or what the police did to me that I went out to demonstrate with my comrades."

He got up and stepped out onto the balcony.

Aunt Neila was crying. Her eyes, accusing, sought out mine.

"I'm so sorry, Auntie Neila, I'm really sorry." It was all I could do to whisper those few words. The blow to my back had cut off the flow of air to my lungs. For a few seconds, I thought I was going to suffocate. Life was rushing out of me. It only lasted a few seconds, but it seemed like an eternity.

"I'm taking you to see Doctor Zarrouk. He's a kind man. I can't leave you like this."

She got up. I wanted to say no, but I knew that this was her way of calming her anxiety and burying the guilt she felt toward Mom and me.

"Your mother would be furious with us if she ever found out what happened!"

Mom's face appeared in front of my eyes. I wasn't at all certain that she would be furious. Worried, yes, but not furious. Maybe she would even be proud to know that I'd joined a demonstration in Tunisia. Me, little Lila who didn't even want to set foot in Tunis to learn a few words of Arabic, suddenly there in the public square with veteran trade unionists chanting political slogans. Who would have believed it?

My phone was vibrating in my purse. It was Donia.

"Call her later," Aunt Neila ordered. "Right now, we're going to see the doctor."

Donia was near hysterical. She felt guilty for losing track of me. But it wasn't her fault; we had been separated by force. I took a blow I hadn't expected. Our hands had parted. The crowd was far more powerful than we were.

My visit to the doctor didn't last long. He ordered a few days' rest. Aunt Neila didn't tell him the truth. She was still frightened. I was in the *souk*, she explained; it was crowded. From the glance the doctor threw her, I could tell he didn't believe her story. But she was right; he was kind. He fell silent for a moment, then smiled and said: "Anything can happen in this country, *rabbi yostor!* Go home and get a good rest."

When I returned to the apartment, two surprises

awaited me. First, Donia was at the door; she wanted to make sure I was all right. The second surprise was even bigger. Mom had left a message on Aunt Neila's phone: she would be arriving tomorrow afternoon on a flight from Paris.

TWENTY-FIVE

Tunis, May, 1984

THE AMERICAN CULTURAL CENTRE had become my life preserver, and I held fast to it with all my strength. Mother never missed an opportunity to scold me, to make me regret my reprehensible behaviour at the *lycée*. She would come into my room and find me stretched out on my bed, or at my desk studying the notes that Neila passed on to me, and exclaim derisively: "What's the point of studying if you can't graduate this summer? Can't you get it through your head? You've been kicked out of the *lycée!*"

At first, I answered by saying: "I'll graduate next year. Papa told me that the *La Réussite* academy would accept me."

"Don't count on it! Do you think your father can

afford the cost of tuition? He'll need a second salary. You should have thought of that before you insulted the instructor in front of the whole class."

"He deserved it, the jerk!" I shot back, eyes filled with tears and voice angrier than ever.

"Well, he may be a jerk, but at least he became a *lycée* instructor. But what did you accomplish with that high-falutin dignity and integrity of yours? Why couldn't you just keep your mouth shut? Answer me! Now you're always around the house. Won't be too long before you end up as a cleaning lady, scrubbing floors and washing walls, that's what's going to become of you!"

She rushed out, slamming the door behind her. I didn't budge from my room. There was no way I could respond to her vicious attacks.

I wept and gnawed at my anger like a cow chewing its cud. Father didn't say a word. TV. Armchair. Silence. That was enough for him.

Neila and Alex were all I had left, and Neila was encouraging me to learn computing.

"My cousin Mariam failed her baccalaureate twice, then she enrolled in a private school, actually a computer science institute. It looks like the thing right now. Why don't you do what she did?"

I was stung to the quick.

"But Neila, it's not the same thing at all. I didn't fail my baccalaureate. They stole my right to take the final exam, that's all there is to it. It's not at all like your cousin's case."

"I know, you're smarter than she is, I admit it. But the result is the same — you didn't pass the exam."

Everybody seemed to be saying that without my baccalaureate, I was worthless, that it was the end of the line for me, that I was on a collision course headed for the wall. In Mother's eyes, I'd never be anything but a cleaning lady, and, for Neila, the best I could hope for would be to learn computing. Father had no career expectations for me. Or if he did, he hadn't said a word about it. Only Alex had confidence in me. And if Mounir hadn't been in prison, he would have encouraged me to keep going, not to give up, to enrol in an other private school and to try my luck the following year. He would have found a way to tell me that I could make it. He would have encouraged me to stand straight, to never bow my head to injustice. He would have talked to Neila, and she would have supported me.

MY RELATIONSHIP WITH Alex was growing stronger by the day. There was no denying it: I loved him. I knew it from the way my heart began to pound whenever I saw him. I knew it from the endless hours I spent daydreaming about him. I knew it from the happiness I felt when I was together with him. But what about him?

He told me nothing of his feelings, but I sensed that he loved me too. Or at least, that he was happy when we were together. Otherwise, why would he have suggested that I go to Canada?

Since our last meeting, Alex had said nothing more about his idea. But it was all I could think of, day and night. The idea was becoming an obsession. How would I get to Canada? On my own? With him? As what? His girlfriend? Everything was mixed up in my head. I made up my mind to clear things up with him.

One day at the cultural centre, as I was about to leave for home and he was going into his office, electric cables in hand, I went up to him.

"Hello, Alex! Still hard at work?"

"Yes, but I'm almost finished. Would you like to talk? We could go for a walk or a bite together. It's such a beautiful day!"

I accepted his invitation. Instead of heading home, I sat down again, book in hand, until he finished his work.

I didn't know whether it was because of most of the people around me were rejecting me, but I was getting more and more attached to Alex by the day. His voice touched me like a caress. His eyes embraced me with gentleness. His smile followed me everywhere in my dreams. Alex had become my dream. The dream that kept me alive. What should I do? Flee from him or flee with him?

Our walk that day was a pleasant one indeed. We first took the bus, then got off at Pasteur Square and walked to the Belvedere. It was a large park, full of tall trees and with a children's merry-go-round and a zoo. I used to go often when I was a little girl. But it had been years since I'd last set foot there. I'd suggested the idea to Alex, and he'd agreed without a moment's hesitation. There, at least, no one would stop us from entering, as the watchman had at Zitouna Mosque. Not to mention that it was a favourite spot for lovers, who could hide there from inquiring eyes.

"Are you hungry?" I suddenly asked Alex, as we passed a *kaki* vendor.

"A little."

I rushed off and bought two small bags of dough balls the size of walnuts, flavored with anise and coarse salt, made in the city's bakeries and sold by street vendors. Sometimes they came in the form of tresses or a round cake.

"What is it?" asked Alex, half-amused, half-concerned, when he saw the two little cellophane bags stuffed full of beige coloured balls.

"It's *kaki*, taste one!"

I opened a package, took out a little ball and handed it to him. The warmth of his hand made me shiver. He crunched the dough ball between his teeth.

"They're a little like chips," he said.

Kaki crumbs drifted down onto his sweater as he continued to chew away like a little boy.

"What are chips?"

"They're a little like *kakis*."

We burst out laughing. Here, in this magnificent public garden, our different homelands and our different cultures were intertwining. Green grass carpeted the brownish-red earth, along with random scatterings of poppies, chamomile, and marigolds. Alex took my hand. I didn't resist. The ancient trees protected us from the inquisitive eyes of passersby. The smell of the eucalyptus, of the mimosas, of the carob trees and the pines perfumed the spring air. I forgot my mother, my father, Neila, Monsieur Kamel, and my expulsion. I breathed in deeply; I felt like Nicole, the heroine of *Tender Is the Night*, alongside Dick. Alex was there beside me. Nothing else mattered.

"Nadia, I don't want to force you, but I have to ask you a question: Will you come back to Canada with me?"

Alex's words brought me back to earth. I turned to face him.

I wanted to answer, "No! How could I ever do such a thing to my parents?" but to my astonishment, I found myself saying: "How am I supposed to come with you? I don't even have a passport."

"The passport's no problem. We can settle all the paperwork. Do you want to or not?"

We were seated on a wooden bench from which one of the back slats had been torn away. Before us, white swans were gliding majestically over the calm waters of the pond. The cries of wild birds from the nearby zoo broke the peaceful urban silence.

I clasped Alex's hand.

"And where would I live in Canada? All alone? I don't know anyone there. The only person I know is you."

Alex smiled.

"But you'd be living with me, of course. What I mean is, we can get married and leave together. And live together."

Marry Alex? Marry a *gaouri*? Neila was right to be suspicious. What would Mother think? Father? The neighbours?

My head was spinning. I wanted to pick up my purse and run. Forget all about Alex. Go back to my room, my bed, my books, to my cozy little cocoon. Go back to being the carefree little girl I was before the couscous revolt. Enrol in a computing academy and pick up my life where I left off. Maybe I could even become a secretary in an office somewhere. Keep my head down.

But something inside me was rejecting the fate that everybody seemed to have planned for me. Something weighty, powerful, as unyielding as an iron ball was struggling to break free from deep within me. It was made up of Mounir's twisted face, Father's terrifying silence, Sonia's spiteful smile, Mother's penetrating eyes, and the deafening sound of bullets on the day of the riots. I'd rejected injustice. I'd rejected the status quo. My expulsion was part of the price I had to pay for my failure to submit. Soon, the rest of the bill would come due. No, I would not be going back to where we began, as Bourguiba had enjoined us on television. There, seated on a wooden park bench, watching the swans glide like dancers waltzing across the water, I decided that my life must change. I knew then that I must make the most important decision of my life: to marry Alex and go with him to Canada.

TWENTY-SIX

Tunis, January 6, 2011

TALK ABOUT A CRAZY story! So, I leave Canada and come to Tunis against my will to learn Arabic and, a few weeks later here I am caught up in a revolution! What next? My mom, who hadn't set foot in Tunisia for years, was about to join me. Who would have believed it? Me, least of all. My back still hurt. Luckily it was nothing serious.

We drove out to greet Mom at Tunis-Carthage Airport. Armoured vehicles lined the streets the entire way. The country was almost in a state of war. Demonstrations had broken out in the poor districts of Tunis.

I wasn't entirely looking forward to the meeting. How would she react to my newest involvement? I had a serious case of nerves. But Aunt Neila and Uncle

Mounir were beside themselves with joy, Aunt Neila
most of all. She couldn't stop talking about Mom, telling me how much she'd missed her.

"You know Lila, I haven't seen your mother since she
left for Canada with your dad. At first, she told us she
was busy with her studies, then with your birth, then
with her work. There was always some reason or other
why she couldn't come back. I spent wonderful years
with your mom. She has a special place in my heart. In
fact, she's irreplaceable."

She turned to her husband, who was driving in
silence.

"Remember, Mounir, before our wedding, how
much I cried because Nadia couldn't be with us?"

He nodded in agreement, then glanced at me in the
rearview mirror: "Your mom did the right thing, leaving. Sure it was tough on us, but they'd unjustly kicked
her out of the *lycée*. She had her future to think about.
And what do you know? It looks like everything worked
out for the best. The tree produced fine fruit. Nadia sent
us our little Lila, a budding revolutionary."

He winked at me. I smiled back.

"Wait a minute! I'm no revolutionary like you. Just
call me a young militant."

He smiled again. Aunt Neila was wriggling with
impatience in her seat.

"Count me out of your group! I'm no revolutionary,

and no militant either. I want peace. Revolutions only bring trouble."

"So what brings freedom?" asked Uncle Mounir.

Aunt Neila said nothing and stared out the car window. I could see her jaw working back and forth nervously. At the airport, Uncle Mounir drove up and down looking for a parking spot; cars were parked every which way. Two policemen were checking a taxi driver's papers. His cab was pulled over to the side of the road.

My heart was beating faster and faster. The inescapable moment when my eyes and Mom's would meet, here, on Tunisian soil, was not far off.

The atmosphere in the terminal was surprisingly quiet. A few passengers were hurrying through the main hall, some arriving, others departing. The country was still unstable. The scene was totally different from all the noise and confusion I'd experienced the month before, when I arrived. Today there were no boisterous tourists, no cleaning ladies with carts, none of the people come to bid someone farewell or to welcome some dear friend or relative. The spirit of revolt had taken over, in peoples' minds and even in public spaces. The terminal building was almost empty. From a distance I heard someone speaking with an American accent. It was a young man heading for the exit. He looked like a journalist, with his laptop in his backpack and his camera equipment in a bag slung over his shoulder. He was talking on his phone. Tunis wasn't attracting many tourists, but it was definitely attracting reporters.

I was lost in thought when Aunt Neila tugged at my sleeve.

"Lila, there's your mom! Oh my God, I can't believe my eyes! Hurry up, Lila, here she comes!"

Mom was making her way toward us. Her wavy hair reached down to her shoulders, and for the first time, I spotted a few strands of grey among her abundant locks. All of a sudden, she seemed very small: about the size of a young woman with her luggage arriving for the first time in a foreign land. The urge to rush toward her, to throw my arms around her, surged over me. But I held back. Aunt Neila did it instead. I stood beside Uncle Mounir. He looked as though he couldn't believe his eyes.

"Nadia, my precious Nadia! How many years has it been since we saw you? You haven't changed a bit. Same eyes, same walk. How badly we've missed you!"

Nadia and Neila embraced, laughing and crying all at once. I waited for a moment of calm between the two friends and came up to Mom. I kissed her on the cheeks, she took me in her arms.

"My darling Lila! I'm so proud of you!"

"Me too, I'm so happy to see you, Mom!"

At last it was Uncle Mounir's turn. There he stood, bolt upright like a sentinel, in front of mom.

"Marhaba bik fi Tounis, ya lilla Nadia! Seems like it's been forever. I never became a lawyer like I hoped, but as you can see, I married the lady of my life and I'm still alive, against all odds."

Mom shook his hand and kissed him on both cheeks. Her tears were still flowing. She couldn't utter a single word.

We made our way slowly to the car. Our return to town was a lively one: Mom, Aunt Neila, and Uncle Mounir couldn't stop talking. I didn't speak. All I could think of were the days to come. What would happen on the streets? I thought of Donia and Jamel; how would their struggle end?

"Someone told me you're involved in politics. Is it true?"

No sooner did I hear Mom's question than my cheeks began to burn.

"Politics? What politics?" I said slowly, weighing my words and trying not to show how agitated I was.

Aunt Neila stifled a nervous laugh.

"Please don't get upset with me, Lila. I mentioned Donia and Jamel and the work you're doing together to your mother. I couldn't keep silent. Nadia knows me too well. I always say what's on my mind."

Now I understood better. Mom knew everything.

She'd come to rescue me from the revolt. She'd come in response to Aunt Neila who was concerned for my safety.

"The truth is, when Neila told me what you were up to with these young people, my first reaction was to feel proud of you. Lila, my own daughter, right in the heart of Tunis, helping young people in their battle against tyranny. I couldn't believe my ears! But then I began to be worry—about you, of course, but also that I might miss the chance to see a revolution happening with my very own eyes, and that's why I dropped everything, jumped on the first flight, and came. Your father couldn't believe my reaction!"

Poor Dad, all alone at home. I missed him too. I would have loved to see him, to hug him, hold his hand spend a minute of silence beside him.

I didn't answer. What was the point? Mom knew everything. But she didn't seem overly concerned either. But a shadow stole over her face: "There's another reason I came back to Tunis." She let out a long sigh, then continued: "My parents. It's time for me to see them again."

TWENTY-SEVEN

Tunis, June 15, 1984

"I'VE MET A YOUNG Canadian, and I'd like you to make his acquaintance." A thousand times over I rehearsed the words in front of the bathroom mirror so that my tongue wouldn't tangle, so that fear wouldn't paralyze my limbs, so that Mother's expression wouldn't make me change my mind at the last minute. I repeated the words in order to be able to deal with my parents' reaction. Rehearsed them there in front of the mirror, hands gripping the edge of the sink as if to prepare myself for the catastrophe that loomed above our family.

At first, Neila didn't agree with my decision.

"Not only did you choose a *gaouri*, but what's more you want to run off with him to Canada! What's gotten into you, Nadia? You've been reading too many books. You've taken leave of your senses!"

"But Alex is nice. He's kind, he's sincere, he loves me, and he wants to help me. Besides, if I go to Canada I'll be able to continue my education. Don't you see Neila? Two birds with one stone! I love Alex, I really love him, and I'm ready to go with him. Plus he's the only one who can truly help me."

Neila's face turned violet; she had a jealous look in her eye.

"But he's not even a Muslim. You're going to marry a Christian? And your children, what religion will they be? Well? Did that ever occur to you, Nadia?"

Once again Neila had put all my ignorance and my naivety on display. I hadn't given such matters a second thought. I had no idea even what Alex's religion was. But how could I possibly marry him in Tunisia if he wasn't a Muslim? How could I have forgotten such a crucial detail?

In my confusion I answered: "I never thought about his religion. All that counts for me is love. And besides — what do you know, anyway? He could just as well become a Muslim. It's only a formality, after all."

Neila shrugged. "It's up to you. He'll have to become a Muslim to marry you. That's what my mother's cousin did. Her husband used to be called Hervé Beaudoin, and when he converted to Islam he changed it, became Hedi

Bouraoui. Mother says he still drinks wine and eats *hallouf.* Just like all the *gaouri.* He only became Muslim for the sake of appearances. Do you think this Alex of yours will do the same thing?"

It was my turn to blush. I was ashamed of myself. Me, who thought I knew everything, who believed that the books I read told me all I needed to know about life. But Neila had the intelligence of the people. She had a simple understanding of things, like my mother. She was a real Tunisian. Now it was beginning to look like I wasn't really enough of one, and before long I wouldn't be one at all.

I spoke to my parents on Sunday.

As on every Sunday, Mother had prepared couscous with lamb and vegetables. It wasn't yet month's end and there was still money in the bank. The atmosphere was relatively upbeat — until the moment I opened my mouth and exploded my bomb.

"What? What are you saying! Now you're talking about a young man, about love! That's all we need right now!"

Mother dropped the long-handled spoon carved from olive wood that she used to scoop the couscous onto our plates. She held her head in her hands and began to weep like a little girl. I'd never seen her that way that before. I almost regretted saying the words. But it was too late. My parents knew my secret now.

"Fatma, please, please, stop," Father muttered in a broken voice. "Fatma, calm down."

Mother didn't want to hear it. She continued to whine like a lamb about to be slaughtered, and then suddenly she said: "Just who is this young man that you want us to meet? A Canadian, is that it? First you make us the laughingstock of the neighbourhood by getting kicked out of the *lycée*, and now you want to lock us up forever? What are you trying to do to your parents, kill us? Send us to the graveyard? Is that what you want? You're not talking. What's the matter, lost your tongue? But you can talk to the boys just fine. And not just any boy, but *gaouri* on top of it! Oh, God in heaven. What have I done in my life to bring us such shame? You are a disgrace, that's what you are!"

Now it was my turn to cry. I wept silently. I didn't want to see my parents so upset, at a loss, not knowing what to do. Papa said nothing. He brought Mother a glass of water into which he put a few drops of orange blossom water. Then he added a bit of sugar, stirred it, and handed her the glass.

"Here, take a swallow, it will make you feel better. Calm down. I'll talk to Nadia. We'll solve the problem."

I crept out on tiptoe and into my room. The couscous was getting cold on the table. My stomach was rumbling, but food was the last thing on my mind. What would become of me now? What would become of my parents?

Before long Father came into my room, his face drained from the shock of the news. He said drily: "So then, who is the boy you want us to meet?"

"He's a young man I met at the American cultural centre. His name is Alexander Martin. He works there as a computer technician. We just chat, like friends. Nothing more."

I couldn't manage to tell Father the whole truth.

"What do you mean, 'like friends'? You know as well as I do that at your age, there's no such thing as innocent friendship between boys and girls. You do know that, don't you?"

"Papa, I swear! There's nothing to be worried about. Alexander has good intentions. He's not trying to hurt me. He only wants to . . . to marry me and take me with him to Canada."

Now Father's face began to darken. I'd never seen him so angry.

"You're only eighteen years old and now you want to marry some foreigner and move to Canada with him? Nadia, what's come over you?"

I searched for words. I found none.

"You think things are that easy? And what about us, your parents? We brought you up, sent you to school. And now you're throwing us into the garbage. You couldn't care less about us, could you?"

"Of course not. Papa, I only wanted you to meet
him..."

He cut me off: "For what? To admire his pretty face?
Tell me why you think I should make the acquaintance
of this Canadian? Are you seriously thinking of marrying him?"

I lowered my eyes. Alex appeared. Was I going to
let everything drop? Or was I going to straighten my
back and shout out the truth, loud and clear? I felt a bit
more confident.

"If I marry him, I could study in Canada. That way,
I'd still have a future."

"And what about our future? Us, your parents! Did
you ever think for even a second about us?"

"I love you Papa, and I don't want to let you down.
My expulsion from the *lycée* was unjust, and you know
it. Alex...Alexander is really nice. He wants to help me.
He wants what's best for me."

"So now you're sticking up for him? Didn't it ever
occur to you that he's a Christian, and that you can't
marry a Christian? Didn't you ever think about that?"

Encouraged by what seemed to be an opening on
Father's part, I ventured: "But he can become a Mus-
lim, Papa. If he's really serious, he'll surely become a
Muslim. I promise you."

Papa said nothing and left the room. I could hear
Mother's wailing. He told her everything.

"I'll kill her, the filthy little insect! Just let me at her, I'll finish her off, once and for all."

Father's voice took over.

"You'll do no such thing. I'll settle this matter. Calm down."

I stayed in my room, too frightened of confronting my parents. I loved Alex. I knew it today when I talked about him in front of my parents. I was in love with a man from another country, who had different values and who belonged to another culture. I was attracted to him, to his smile, his eyes, his calm, and his courtesy. Everything about him drew me toward him. But what else did I know about him? Nothing, next to nothing. Maybe he'd get tired of me once we'd made it to Canada. Maybe he would beat me. Maybe he would drop me. With a Tunisian husband I'd always have my parents to fall back on if things worked out badly. But if I went off with Alex to Canada and he turned out to be nasty or mean, I would be up against him all by myself. Nobody would come to my defense.

I could hear Mother's wails coming from the kitchen; they were like hammer blows crushing my bones. Mother was hardly my closest ally these days. The way she reacted to my expulsion from the *lycée* had almost been too much for me to bear. Seeing her in such a state made me feel miserable and guilty. Yes, I was the reason for her unhappiness. Her unhappiness came from seeing her only daughter crumble before her very eyes like an ancient relic. I suffered, too, for my father. Torn between paternal love and the authority he'd never truly been able to assume, today he seemed even more defenseless than ever.

Still holed up in my room, writhing with chagrin, I could only bring one image to mind: that of Alex, and me beside him, walking through the *medina* after our aborted visit to the Zitouna Mosque. Only Alex could understand my sadness; only Alex offered me an escape from injustice. I would not let him down. I would overcome my fears and set myself free from the shackles that bound me, that held me back from my march toward freedom. A new plan was taking shape in my mind. I would leave with Alex, whatever the price. I would flee with him. My mind was made up. No one would stop me. Least of all my parents.

TWENTY-EIGHT

Tunis, January 11, 2011

I MET MY GRANDPARENTS for the first time the day that unrest peaked in the poor districts of Tunis. Ettadamoun Township was aflame; blood was flowing in the streets.

Mom, who never talked about her parents except to say that they were old and that they lived outside of Tunis, surprised me when she announced that we were going to visit them. Should I have attributed the silence to my indifference or to the scant enthusiasm she always showed toward her father and mother? Both, perhaps?

"Where do they live?" I asked with curiosity.

"Tebourba. A charming little town with an ancient history. There's good agricultural land and the people are kind and simple," she replied, her eyes damp.

We were in downtown Tunis, in Barcelona Square. There were police at every corner. As our taxi carried us toward the Central Station, where we'd catch a bus, I caught sight of an army tank stationed in front of a tall building. We waited for the bus, which gave no sign of appearing. Mom avoided my gaze. Her tired eyes sought out the blue bus that Uncle Mounir had strongly advised us to take, and which was now late.

"My parents settled in Tebourba after... after I went to Canada. My father renovated his parents' old home and they moved there," she finally explained. The words came out with difficulty.

"Why didn't you ever tell me anything? Why didn't you ever tell me about your parents? You only talked about Aunt Neila and Uncle Mounir. Why did you want me to learn Arabic in Tunisia when you, who grew up there, didn't even stay in touch with your roots?"

Without noticing, I'd raised my voice. The odd passerby turned to stare at us. The suffocating smell from the exhaust fumes of the buses entering and leaving the station filled the air. I felt dizzy. My lungs were calling for help.

"It wasn't my choice. My parents never accepted that I was going to marry your father. They didn't want to see me again. It broke my heart, but there was nothing left for me but to leave. Thankfully Neila would give me their news. I didn't want to say anything to you. I didn't want you to hold it against them for rejecting your dad. Today, I think the time has come to see them. I'm taking you with me. Maybe they'll forgive me."

Forgive her for choosing her husband? I wanted to ask another question. Too late. A crowd had converged in front of the blue bus that had just pulled up in front of us. Mom pushed me gently forward; we had to move quickly to get a seat. Luckily we found two places. Seated side by side, we waited in silence for the bus to move.

I watched the landscape rush by, like so many photographs from a magazine. A tree bent over the highway. A donkey cart. A decrepit factory. Two men slogging along the roadside, as though in a dream, staring off into the distance, nothing connecting them, one following the other.

"Is it far to Tebourba?" I asked, to break the silence.

"About twenty miles. You'll see. It's a lovely place. Tebourba is an ancient Roman city—Thuburdo Minus, that was its Roman name. There were even Christian martyrs there, during the early years of Christianity in Africa. Then came the Moors from Andalusia fleeing the Spanish Inquisition. They settled there and built the city that we see today. You'll see. It's a magnificent place."

It was the same enthusiasm I'd gotten used to when

she would praise her country to the skies back in Canada. An enthusiasm that replaced the fatigue of jet lag I could still see on her face. She'd never told me the story. That dark part of her life that she'd kept so well hidden in our calm and humdrum Canadian daily routine.

"Did you ever visit Tebourba?" I asked her, at last.

"A few times, when I was a little girl. But when my grandparents died, may God bless their souls, my father closed the house . . . until I left for Canada, that is."

She stopped, pulled out a hanky, and wiped her eyes. I looked out the window. Now the road ran parallel to a river.

Mom put away her hanky, and exclaimed, pointing to the riverbanks: "Look! It's the Medjerda, the Tunisian Saint Lawrence!"

I smiled. Mom too. We had the same references. Canada had separated Mom from the land of her birth, and suddenly it popped back up, bringing us together in a blue bus as we went searching for our roots.

"Thanks to the waters of this river, this region one of the most fertile in the country." Mom went on.

She didn't have time to finish her sentence. We had already arrived. From far off I could see a monument surrounded by a small garden bordered by a black-painted fence.

At the bus station, Mom seemed a bit lost. Police cars were everywhere. The revolution was alive among the people. I shivered. The place was teeming with ambulant vendors: men hawking bread, vegetables, and cigarettes. People milled around. Motorcycles were heading in all directions. I observed the human scene with curious eyes. Discreetly, Mom approached an elderly gentleman sitting beside a table, a glass of tea in his hand. The frail-looking man, wearing a *chéchia* to cover his sparse white hair, pointed out a street to her.

"Lila," exclaimed Mom, taking me by the hand, "it's this way. I can't recognize a thing. Everything has changed. Luckily the man knew where our house is."

We walked down a street that ended in an alleyway. We had to step over a garbage bag torn open by some animal. Ahead of us, a skinny cat skittered across the road. At the end of the alley stood a tiny mosque with a green dome. And there, to our left, a house. We came to a stop in front of a red-painted door with a sky-blue frame. Two crumbling stone columns framed the doorway, which was decorated with two brass knockers. My Mom grasped one of them.

We waited a moment. An eternity. An elderly gentleman opened the door. He could only be my grandfather. He had Mom's forehead, a forehead just like mine. He stared at us for a few seconds, squinting in an effort to figure out what was happening.

"Papa, it's me, Nadia, your daughter."

Without waiting for the elderly gentleman's reaction,

she threw herself into his arms. I stood there, off to one side, not knowing what to do with my hands or my emotions.

The elderly gentleman—my grandfather—turned toward me. Smiled at me. There were gaps in his teeth. He leaned in my direction and then, in shaky French, as he beckoned to me, he said: "Come closer, my little one. You must be Lila. Oh my God! How long I've waited for this moment!"

He embraced me. I kissed him clumsily on the cheek. A broad smile lit up his wrinkled face.

An elderly lady, her hair carefully arranged, came to the door. My Mom hastily threw her arms around her. It was my grandmother. She looked startled. There was confusion in her eyes. She could not understand the strange scene that was unfolding on her doorstep.

"Fatma, come over here! It's Nadia and her daughter, Lila. Didn't I tell you time and again that she would come back? I knew it—my heart would never betray me, I knew she would come back one day. Today is that day. Glory to God!"

TWENTY-NINE

Ottawa, July 2, 1984

Dear Neila,

Who would ever have believed that one day I'd be writing you a letter from Canada? I'm living in Ottawa, the capital of this huge country that still scares me. Me, Nadia, the naive little girl who thought Canada only existed in adventure movies. But look! It's all true. I'm writing you from that very same country. Perhaps you're still angry with me, because I let you down. Look, I didn't have any choice. It was Tunisia that let me down. No, not Tunisia; the Tunisians let me down. Monsieur Kamel, Sonia, my own mother, the lycée, the regime, the police . . . They did everything they could to shove me aside, to put me down. I didn't have any other choice. I had to leave. I left my country with a heavy heart, a heart as big as a watermelon. Remember those long green watermelons like sagging breasts we used to see laid out for sale along the country roads, or piled high in Peugeot 404 pickup trucks? The ones we'd eat on the hottest days and the gritty pink juice would dribble down our chins? We laughed and wiped our mouths with our hands. Then we went after the black seeds; we chewed through the shells with our teeth and sucked the white seeds hiding inside. And spend the whole day telling stupid stories. How carefree we were! No more, Neila. We've become cynical and bitter. We've become adults.

I crept out like a thief leaving a store he's robbed. I left the country I love and the people I love to live with the man I love. It was hard, Neila. Maybe you'll never forgive me; it's true, I left in secret. I went with Alex. But he never touched me before we were married. I committed no sin, I swear on my father's head. "Ib!" was what mother always said about the things she disapproved of. I guess I committed plenty of ibs in her eyes. On the other hand, Alex became a Muslim. He took the Shahada in front of an imam. And don't be suspicious! He doesn't drink wine and eat pork like that guy Hedi Bouraoui, your mother's cousin's husband. The same imam who witnessed his conversion

*married us. Am Salam, that was his name. A poor
imam we met in the Tunis souk. We searched for
hours looking for someone who would listen to us and
believe us. A Tunisian girl and a Canadian man.*

*We registered our marriage at Tunis City Hall. The
registrar gave me an accusatory look. "Ya binti, why
are you marrying this Christian? There are still plenty
of good Muslim boys in this town. Why are you doing
this? He only converted to marry you. He's not doing
it for God, but for you. That's no good." He whispered
those words to me, and then handed me the papers
as he waited for my answer. But I said nothing. Alex
wanted to know what the man had said. "Nothing.
He was wishing us good luck." Alex smiled weakly;
he was nobody's fool.*

*You know how our compatriots are, Neila. They stick
their noses into everything. The clerk at city hall was
no exception. When I went walking with Alex along
the street I could hear the men whispering: "Look at
the little whore! That's the way our girls end up. Selling themselves to some gaouri!"*

*I cried at night when I remembered those words. And
you know something, Neila, I wasn't strong enough to
answer back. Fear has tied our tongues. The same fear*

that Botti made us suck like a bitter candy. With all the power of a glance, and the violence of a word. And along with fear, comes shame. The feeling of shame follows me wherever I go, right down to the depths of my being.

It took a few weeks before I could get a visa. Alex arranged everything: our airplane tickets, our documents, everything! A remarkable guy! I'm sure Mounir will make you happy, just as Alex is making me happy.

There was no embroidered gown at my wedding. No henna on my hands. No deafening band. No bottles of soda pop served on trays tilted to one side from the weight. Nothing. Not even a goodbye from my parents. It broke my heart. I ask you to give them my greetings. I'll come to see them when things get better.

Yesterday was Canada's national holiday. The day Canada became a real country. A bit like Independence Day back home, except in Tunisia everybody stays home. There's nothing to celebrate. Everybody was happy because it was the beginning of spring vacation. Then we'd watch the news on TV with their boring military parades and the dignitaries shaking hands. Here, it's not like that at all. Alex and I went to the Canadian parliament. It's a handsome building, the equivalent of our own Bardo. Except that when it comes to size, there's no comparison. It's got a tall tower with a clock at the top and a green copper roof. A joyful crowd came to celebrate the birth of their country. Alex is so considerate. We're living in an apartment close to the University of Ottawa. Alex works in a computer store. He found a job right away. No need for relations. No need for connections. It's totally different from back home. He just sent in his CV, and they called him for an interview.

I miss you, Neila. I miss life in Tunisia. The monotony of everyday life. Our little squabbles and our fits of laughter. My folks too. Mother says she doesn't have a daughter any more. Papa says nothing. Instead of words, now, there's silence. Do you ever see my parents? What do they say? One day, if I ever have a daughter, I'll name her Lila. Your favourite colour. Remember how you used to dance to Gérard Lenorman's song "Lila"? We must have been twelve years old. You whirled like a spinning top until you flopped down on the bed, dizzy. I couldn't stop you. Do you still remember all that silliness, Neila? I remember everything! When Alex is at work and I'm feeling sad, I close my eyes and remember all that. And my sadness dissolves like salt in water. I cry, too, but I don't say a word to Alex. *I don't want him to see me unhappy, but deep down, I think he knows. He doesn't say a word. He kisses me on the mouth and I feel like staying in his arms forever.*

It's funny for me to be telling you all this, the girl who taught me all there was to know about boys. Me, who thought you'd get married before me for sure! Me, who was a little jealous to see you so happy with Mounir! Do you have any news from him? When will they release him? Do you ever see his little brother Mohamed? Just between us, I told Alex the whole story. He told me we could do something about it from here. There's an Amnesty International office in Ottawa. It's a human rights organization. They help imprisoned people everywhere in the world. They fight against torture. I'll go see them and talk to them about the repression in Tunisia. I'll tell them about Mounir, his political activities, and his unjust arrest. Who knows? Maybe they can do something about it. Maybe he'll be set free.

Ah, I almost forgot the good news! I'm sure you'll be happy for me! I'm going back to school, at a lycée. A real one, Neila. Here they call it a "collegiate institute." Mine is called Lisgar. I'd never heard of it before. For sure, they have some weird names here. Yes, I'm going back to school, but all in English. It will be hard, but I think I can do it. One day, those nobodies who kicked me out of the lycée *in Tunis will be sorry. I'll show them what I can do! I can hear you laughing. Are you making fun of me? You think I'm silly, don't you? Don't worry about it; I love it when you laugh. It makes me want to dream, it keeps me alive. In fact, I only live to dream.*

Love and kisses,
Your dear friend Nadia

THIRTY

Tunis, January 13, 2011

TWO DAYS WITH MY grandparents. Two days of tears and laughter. Two days when the past married the present to give birth to me: Lila, the Canadian, the Tunisian, the hybrid, the incomprehensible dream. Time heals all wounds, they say. I'm not so sure. I didn't even have a past. Only the present counted for me. But all at once, gaping wounds opened up in my heart. One after another, like shots fired in quick succession. My mother's flight, her marriage to my father, meeting my grandparents.

They lived a modest life in their old Arab-style house: two tiny rooms, a kitchen, and an inner courtyard. No bathroom, just a miniature squat toilet with a sink so small you could barely wash your hands, and above it a mirror stained from the damp.

"Don't they take showers here, or what?" I asked Mom, a little disturbed by the primitive facilities.

I'd spoken softly to avoid being overheard, but grandma's antennae picked up my voice.

"What does your daughter want?" she asked, glancing at Mom with an inquisitive smile.

Grandma talked to Mom like a guest she was trying to please. She was still treading gingerly. With each word, each silence, each glance, the past would come rushing back. She didn't wait for an answer, and Mom was still looking for the right words. In a mixture of Arabic and French, which I easily understood, she said: "You want...shower? I put on water to heat. You shower in toilet..."

Mom interrupted politely. "Lila doesn't really need to take a shower. She only wants to know where you usually take one. Don't bother, *Ommi*, no need to heat water. She had a shower yesterday at Neila's."

Then she told me: "Lila, Arab houses don't usually have a bathroom, because people go to the *hammam*. There's one at every street corner, daytime for men, evenings for women and children."

I'd asked a simple question. Now I was getting more information than I could assimilate.

Meanwhile, Mom couldn't stop kissing her parents. Once on the right cheek, once on the left cheek, once on the forehead, and once on the right hand. I found my granddad Ali polite and gentle. He spoke to me in French, which irritated his wife, because she couldn't understand every word. It was one of those rare times when he could get the better of her.

Grandma Fatma wasn't mean, but I did find her a little excessive in the way she looked at you, the way she talked, the way she expressed her feelings.

The room where we spent our first night together also made do as a living room. There were two wooden beds, both a kind of narrow sofa bed with armrests and a backrest. They were decorated with little cushions. A foam mattress covered with the same fabric as the cushions provided enough space to sit down comfortably and even to stretch out. In the middle of the room was a low table with a vase full of plastic flowers. An outsize painting—a lugubrious still life—covered most of one wall. I wondered just where my grandparents had found such a monstrosity. An old television set stood in one corner, and next to it, shelves full of worn-out books. Atop those same shelves was a photo of me as a baby—I must have been two or three—in Andrew Haydon Park, in Ottawa, staring at the wild geese.

The entire evening, all Mom could do was ask questions. My grandparents did their best to answer. "Whatever became of little Najwa?" Mom asked Grandma Fatma.

"She never finished school. Hedia, her mother, could

never make ends meet, even with the money her poor husband left her when he died. Six children, what can you do? So Najwa got married to a doctor who went to work in Saudi Arabia. She came to see us once or twice. Really put on weight. It was hard for her even to move around. But she was just as affectionate as ever."

Mom seemed disappointed by Najwa's story; her eyes turned sad once more. Grandma Fatma went on: "Next time she comes to see me, I'll ask her to talk to you over the computer. Everybody uses *skee* or *skibe* or something like that. You talk to the computer and the other person answers you. I saw our neighbour talking to her son who lives in France. Here, all we have is a telephone, and it barely works."

She glanced at the timeworn set, which looked like a relic from an old film. It sat atop a small table in one corner of the room.

Mom responded: "That's a good idea. Ask her to call me on Skype, that's what they call it. I loved Najwa. How I'd like to talk to her after all these years. We'd have so much to tell each other."

I was having trouble keeping track of what they were saying. I didn't know Najwa or any of the other people whose names kept popping up in the lively conversation between Mom and her parents.

I thought of my dad. Why had these people — my mother's own family — rejected him? Why did they never accept him as a son-in-law? And, as though Grandma had read my thoughts, she surprised me when she said: "*Ya Lila*, you look just like your mother, like two drops of water, except for your eyes, they're your father's. He must feel so alone, that poor Iskander. You left him to fend for himself, you and your mother. No wife to prepare his meals, no daughter to keep him company."

Her eyes were glinting maliciously. I couldn't tell whether she was being sincere or sarcastic. Mom, whose face tensed at the sound of the Arabic version of my dad's name, suddenly relaxed. Grandma's question, sincere or not, had touched the secret doorway, the one everyone was thinking about, the one that put everybody on edge.

"Alex is doing just fine, *Ommi*. I left him plenty of food in the freezer. And what's more, he's a good cook. He can look after himself just fine. A few more days, and we'll all be together, *insha'Allah*."

Grandma was surprised, and her curious look gave her away: "What does he know how to cook, anyway? Tagines, soups, couscous? Does he know our cooking?"

"He knows everything. We learned together. I remembered the things I used to eat when I was a little girl and I tried to prepare them, and he helped me out."

Fatma was wide-eyed. Granddad dropped in a word: "One day, he'll come and sample one of your delicious dishes, *ya* Fatma!"

She fell silent; it was as though she already regretted that Granddad had gone so far.

The little heater in the middle of the living room cast its flickering blue light over us. The atmosphere was sweet and melancholy at the same time; Mom leaned over toward her mother and took her in her arms. A long, touching embrace. I could feel the tears running down my cheeks. Granddad stepped outside. I watched his shadow move along one of the walls. Then he slowly disappeared in the darkness.

THIRTY-ONE

Ottawa, April 4, 1992

Dear Neila,

Thanks for your last letter. Nothing but good news all around! I'm so happy to learn that they finally released Mounir. Unbelievable! Held for more than seven years for daring to say no to injustice. I cried when I saw your wedding photo. You can't imagine how happy I am for both of you. At last the dream of a lifetime is coming true. You're just wonderful in the photo. Exactly like a movie star. Your hair so elegant, your cheeks all powdered, and your eyes made up. I swear, you look just like Claudia Cardinale when she was young. And Mounir, he hasn't changed a bit. He's still just as serious as I remember him when I saw him at the entrance to the shopping centre searching customers' bags. Ah, my dearest Neila, the years are passing like the waves of the sea, but suffering sinks to the bottom.

You wrote that my parents attended your marriage, and I could feel my heart leap. You know well that you were always like a second daughter to them. Your wedding was the one I could never give them. Papa answered two or three of my letters. Mother doesn't even want to talk to me on the phone. I wrote to Papa in my letters that I wanted to speak to her. I gave him my number here in Ottawa, but heard nothing; she's still turning her back on me. Even when I graduated from university, with my degree in English literature, she didn't budge an inch. Papa only tells me the barest minimum — a few words and the letter is over. I read it and reread it to give myself the impression that he's still talking to me. The only time I detected a note of pride was when I announced that I'd gotten my university degree. It was like a faint ray of light over a dark and stormy sea. Only a single sentence that said: "I always knew you were a good student." Maybe mother will speak to me one day. When she learns I'll soon be a mother, maybe she'll change her mind. I keep on hoping.

It's true. I didn't tell you right away: I can feel the baby moving around in my tummy. This is a kind of happiness I've never experienced before, a feeling that life is taking shape inside me, helping me to forget the pain of being parted from my parents. Alex is beside himself with joy. He'll soon be a father. Always the same old guy: sweet tempered and lovable. Ah, if only my parents would accept him! Actually, it's not so much him as it is the rebellious girl I became after the couscous revolt. They could never come to terms with the new Nadia. The ghost of the old Nadia still hovers over their life. Docile Nadia, the little girl who didn't ask too many questions, the little girl who was ready to be just like everybody else, the little girl who would pass the baccalaureate exams with honors and become the pride of the neighbourhood.

Just look at me! Stirring up bitter memories! I try to forget, to move on, but you know just how hard that can be.

I didn't tell you that we've just bought a house. A house like the ones we used to see in the movies. A red brick house with a pitched roof. You won't find anything like it in Tunis. There's a wood floor, a fireplace in the living room, and no French doors at all. The windows let in the dazzling Canadian winter light that fills our lives with warmth and hope. I hope you'll come here to Ottawa for a visit. I miss you. All those lost years. Pray for me and for my little Lila who keeps on kicking me in the side.

With all my love,
Nadia

THIRTY-TWO

Tunis, January 14, 2011

WHEN WE LEFT MY grandparents' house, a part of me wanted to stay. Their simple life, Granddad's gentleness, and Grandma's clever mind—everything about them appealed to me. And something drew me to them, too. My own origins in all likelihood. "The power of blood," was what Mom called it. She must be right.

I was in no position to judge my grandparents for having rejected Mom's marriage and hasty departure. All I wanted to do was to savour every moment I spent with them. How futile it was to go back over the past, to criticize my mother for hiding so many things from me. I would have all the time I needed to talk with her when we got back to Ottawa. But for the time being, things were not going well in Tunis. Donia called me

on the morning of our departure from Tebourba. She
was weeping; I could barely understand her. When I
finally figured out what she was saying, I didn't want to
believe her. Jamel had been arrested. Donia was frantic.
I tried to reassure her over the phone, and I promised
to go to see her as soon as we got back to the city.

A few hours later, we met at Uncle Mounir and
Aunt Neila's apartment. Our pleasure after a day and a
half with our family was disturbed now by the flow of
events sweeping the country.

The news of Jamel's arrest shook us all, but it hit
Uncle Mounir hardest. It made him think back to his
own arrest and to his ordeal in Tunisia's prison.

"The guards treated us like cattle. They crowded us
into one cell for hours. If anyone was brave enough to cry
out or to denounce those terrible conditions, he would
be punished. They deprived us of food for whole days."

Aunt Neila was preparing tea in the kitchen, while
Uncle Mounir talked with Mom about the political
situation. Donia's messages kept popping up on my
phone, one after another. During the night they'd taken
Jamel to the police station in his neighbourhood. His
neighbours had alerted Donia to his arrest. At first she
thought it was a rumour, but she soon realized it was
true. Jamel was being held somewhere, either at the
Ministry of the Interior or at a police station. Ettadamoun Township was a battlefield. Dozens had been

injured in clashes between police and demonstrators. Donia was beside herself. Message after message. I had to go to see her, to stand by her. She told me about a mass demonstration in the streets of Tunis.

You'll come with me, won't you? she insisted in her text message.

I had no idea how Mom and her friends would react if I suggested that we all go together. I was afraid they would refuse.

We've got to come out, to denounce injustice! wrote Donia.

I'd love to, but what about Mom and her friends; were they ready to make the leap, ready to defy the regime? Tell them or keep quiet? Eyes focused on my telephone, my heart beat in unison with Donia's. My thoughts were rushing. What would I have to lose if I asked them to come out with Donia and me?

When I spoke, I found I was almost shouting. "Donia says there's going to be a huge demonstration in front of the Ministry of the Interior. She's going to attend and I'm going with her."

I'd hardly finished my sentence when Mom spoke up: "A demo in Tunis! I must be dreaming!"

"We've got to go," Uncle Mounir replied immediately.

"The police will never let people demonstrate. Ben Ali will bring his people out, you'll see!" Aunt Neila's words were a damper upon us. She placed her sunglasses on the table.

"He's nothing to be afraid of," Uncle Mounir said. "Just an old cop ready to collect his pension."

Mom laughed. "You're right, Mounir. What do we have to be afraid of, after all the deaths, all the arrests. We've got to go!"

I was ecstatic. Mom was with us, and Uncle Mounir too. Aunt Neila didn't have a choice. Her fear would soon melt; I could feel it coming.

So, you're coming to the protest? We have to do it, for Jamel, and for all the others! Donia's messages were snapping at my heels, like a rabid dog. I needed a few minutes. Mom and her friends were about to make the decision they could never have made a few years before.

Mom and Uncle Mounir looked Aunt Neila right in the eye. She turned away and stared out the window.

"Okay! I'm coming with you. But you know something? I'm doing it for one person, and one person only." She turned to me, came up to me, and took my hand. "I'm doing it for Lila. She's the future, she's the one who came to change my life. I'm coming out with you, but I'm doing it for her."

Her eyes weren't sad any longer. They were shining, in fact. I threw myself into her arms. Aunt Neila hugged me; I felt as if I would never leave her again.

I'm coming with you. Mom, Aunt Neila, and Uncle Mounir are coming too. We'll stop by to pick you up. I tapped out my message to Donia, not sure whether all of this was real or I was dreaming.

An hour later, we were all crammed into Uncle Mounir's car. I was in the middle, in the back seat, Donia on one side, Mom on the other. Uncle Mounir was behind the wheel, and Aunt Neila was in the passenger seat. We were driving through the back streets, heading for the city centre.

"We should park anywhere we can near Avenue Bourguiba," warned Donia, as she checked her messages. "Our pals are saying that the crowd is getting bigger by the minute."

From my place on the back seat I could see Aunt Neila's taut features. She must have been really nervous. Mom was as happy as a little girl who'd just found a precious object she was sure she'd lost. Energy was flowing up through her roots. She looked out the car window. People were hurrying along the sidewalks. Impassive, the palm trees were barely swaying.

"I'm going to park here," said Uncle Mounir, turning to look at us.

It was a narrow side street. The car seemed to sink, then rise again: the pavement was full of potholes. Grey-painted buildings lined the way, their shuttered French doors opened onto balconies protected by wrought iron railings. There was a grocery store at the corner. The owner was lowering the blind with a crank until the metal barrier locked into position with a clunk.

"Things don't look good," he said, glancing at Uncle Mounir, who locked the car and stuffed the keys into his pocket.

"Looks like there's a big demonstration in front of the Ministry of the Interior, on Avenue Bourguiba," the mustachioed grocer went on, muttering. "That's all I need. I'm closing up shop and going home. I don't like trouble, it's no good for business."

Uncle Mounir answered with a wave of the hand. I walked alongside Donia; Mom fell into step with Aunt Neila and Uncle Mounir.

"I really wanted for Jamel to be with us," sighed Donia. "He dreamed that the people would come out by the thousands. I hope they're not abusing him."

"Don't worry Donia. I'm sure it's all a mistake. They'll let him out sooner or later."

"A mistake! What are you saying? It's a police state here. They'd even arrest a fly on the tiniest suspicion."

Sheepishly I stopped talking. My ignorance continued to startle me. But Donia pretended to take my arguments seriously. She looked at me and smiled, as if to reassure me.

"One of his friends is in critical condition. He was shot in the chest as he was leaving his house. They say there are snipers on the rooftops and hiding behind the shutters of buildings, shooting at random to frighten people. I just now read it on Sami's Facebook page."

"But who does that benefit?" I asked, incredulous, looking around me at the windows of the neighbouring buildings.

"The dictator and his accomplices, that's who! They don't want things to change. They want people to hole up in their burrows, like rabbits, like that grocer we just passed. Did you see the fear on his face? What a wimp!"

I couldn't help grinning. Donia was always quick-witted, even at the worst of times.

I didn't know how, but suddenly we found ourselves on the main street of Tunis: Avenue Bourguiba. Grand as always, like a bride on her wedding day. We'd come out onto it from a side street, Rue Marseille.

Men, women, the old and the young, everyone was marching along the broad avenue between the rows of trees. Some were laughing while others, more serious, were waving homemade placards. On some was written *Ben Ali dégage!*

I turned toward Mom. She was walking arm in arm with Aunt Neila, two little girls who were best friends and never wanted to be separated again. Mom was reliving the couscous revolt that had slipped through her fingers without her ever really being a part of. Today, back in Tunis after more than twenty years, she'd come to do what she could not when she was my age. Uncle Mounir was taking photos with his phone. He was experiencing today's uprising in another way. The previous time, he'd paid with his freedom. Today, he felt proud to be a part of the crowd, and of the feeling that — just maybe — this time would be it.

Donia's eyes were glued to her phone.

"People are coming from all directions," she said. "The end of the regime is not far away. Bouazizi's blood won't have been shed in vain. The blood of the martyrs of all these years won't have been shed in vain. If we're here today, it's because of their sacrifice."

I nodded, almost by reflex. The crowd was heading for the Ministry of the Interior. The immense building, which looked more like a bunker, was ringed by barbed wire. A young woman had scaled one the lampposts that lined the street. The crowd was hysterical. Crying out. And I was crying out along with it. I had no idea what I was saying, but the syllables poured joyously from my mouth to mingle with the roar that filled the entire space.

Although I knew none of the faces I encountered, I felt safe, protected. A sense of calm enveloped me. Perhaps it was the trees that lined the boulevard that formed a natural shield. Those wise old ficus trees with their dense green foliage where tiny sparrows nested protected us.

Suddenly I heard someone cry out: *"Dégage!"* At first it was like a distant murmur, then it became a deep growl. Rolling thunder drawing gradually closer. Euphoria swept over the crowd. I felt as though my lungs would burst. People lifted their arms high in a rapid movement that called upon an invisible interlocutor to clear out. Now the crowd was infuriated. Our hands touched. The people had had enough of the dictatorship. Mom, Aunt Neila, Uncle Mounir, Donia—we were all together, hands raised high above our heads, staring down the looming hulk of the Ministry of the Interior. Our voices merged. The dictator no longer had a choice. He had to abandon power.

That night, back in Aunt Neila's living room, all eyes glued to the television, we learned that the crowd so terrified Ben Ali that he'd fled. I couldn't believe it. It all happened so fast. Maybe he would try to make a comeback. No one knew. Was it at last the end of a long ordeal for the Tunisian people? I had no idea. My friends' struggle had borne fruit. How happy I was that I had added my voice to that of the oppressed. It wasn't much; but doing nothing was not an option.

THIRTY-THREE

Ottawa, January 20, 2011

Dear Donia,

Mother and I are back safely in Ottawa. We had a smooth trip. No surprises. No excitement. The whole way I couldn't stop thinking about you, about Jamel, and about the future of Tunisia. That's where I left my heart. The first thing I did when I got back was to turn on my computer and check Facebook. They released Jamel! What great news! I couldn't believe my eyes. I read and reread the blurb a dozen times. "Jamel Zitouni has been released!" You must be very happy! I'm happy for you. Things still look fragile to me, but I'm confident that a new day will dawn soon for Tunisia.

*Outside, it's snowing and the weather is cold. A dry,
cutting cold like the blade of a sword. But the cold
is my childhood, my life; I can't live without it. I see
the snowflakes dancing up and down like tiny balls
of cotton wool whirling in the air before falling to the
ground in a rush. Their whiteness reminds me of the
rooftops of Tunis, all whitewashed to reflect the burning rays of the sun. It makes me homesick. I'm going
to take some time off, relax for a while, and then get
back to my writing. My courses have started up again.
I'm a little behind, but it was worth every minute.
Imagine! For so long I refused to go to Tunisia! Everything scared me: the people, the language, the environ-
ment, the bright sun beating down on my head. So
there I was, in my egotistical solitude and comfort.
But that's over and done with, Donia. I'm not the
same person. Tunisia changed me. Aunt Neila, Uncle
Mounir, my grandparents, you and Jamel, and even
Am Mokhtar, that old fox — all those people opened
my eyes to another reality, to the struggle for justice,
perseverance, and dignity. Wasn't that what the young
people on Avenue Bourguiba were calling for? I heard
it in their voices and I saw it in their eyes. I shouted
it out along with them. It was a journey that enabled
me to know others, but also to learn who I was. To
learn my story. My own roots. And, of course, to learn
about my mother. I would never have known a thing*

about any of that if I hadn't gone back to the source.
If I hadn't taken the trouble to get my hands dirty,
as the saying goes. And just look at what I came up
with, Donia! Rich, black, fertile soil? I wish I knew.
Only time will tell.

I've started studying psychology at university. I want
to understand people better, to find out how they think,
why they're sometimes nice and sometimes nasty. Why
they act the way they do. I want to continue the search
that began in a sophisticated café in Tunis. Remember,
Donia? The day I met Jamel and your group of friends.
That was the day that I broke out of my little bubble
and realized that there were young people who were
different from me, but who dreamed of freedom and
justice. Anyway, I didn't get it right away, but today,
far from all of you—thousands of miles away!—I'm
sure of it. My heart is calling out loud and clear: I've
changed, Donia, and the main reason is you!

I hear on the news that there is still violence in Tunisia.
I hope your neighbourhood is spared. I still remember
how frightened we were after the huge demonstra-
tion on January 14 and the declaration of a curfew.
Uncle Mounir went out every night to help the men
in the local committees to make sure the citizens were
protected. All the men, young and old, carried sticks

as thick as snake heads to defend themselves against the criminals and the bandits who took control of the streets and set up a reign of terror. All of a sudden the police, who were everywhere in the streets when I arrived in Tunis, disappeared. They were certainly worried that the people would take revenge. Why am I telling you all this? You know much better than I do what happened. Maybe it's because I want to hold onto the memory of those instants. After nightfall, for several days in succession, Aunt Neila, Mom, and I were alone in the apartment. They told me stories about their adolescence, about their parents. I discovered a whole new world.

This summer I intend to come to see you in Tunisia. We'll plan a program. I won't be coming to learn Arabic. Definitely not! My ears are still ringing. And my training was more than I needed. No, I want to go to Sidi Bouzid, to Siliana, to Gafsa, to Tozeur, and to the other towns of the interior. I know it will be hot, but I'd like to visit those towns, the ones that were left behind. I'd like to do something for those people. You see, I owe them something. I owe them the peace that I've found at last.

Hope to see you soon,
Lila

ACKNOWLEDGEMENTS

I thank my translator, Fred A. Reed, and my friend Caroline Lavoie for her critical reading. Her advice, corrections, and suggestions both assisted and inspired me. Thanks as well to my parents. Without their love and their confidence, I would not be what I am today. And last but not least, I thank my husband and my children for their patience.

GLOSSARY

al-Maududi and *Sayed Qutb*	respectively sub-continental and Egyptian Muslim scholars of the mid-twentieth century, often considered ideologists of Salafism
Allahu Akbar. La Ilaha ila'Allah	"God the Almighty! There is no God but God!" the final words of the *athan*, the Muslim call to prayer
Ana uhibu al lughat al Arabiya	"I just love the Arabic language!"
Aunt and *Uncle*	in North Africa "aunt" and "uncle", in addition to their common meaning, are used to describe parents' friends, with no other connotation than affection or respect
binti	literally "my daughter", used by older men when addressing a young girl
botti	fatso, in Tunisian dialect
briks	a savory dish made from fine round sheets of pastry dough containing tuna, grated cheese, capers and a raw egg; the pastry is folded over and fried in hot oil
chéchia	a typically Tunisian men's knit cap; smaller than the fez, and less prestigious socially

Destourian Party	founded by Tunisia's first president Habib Bourguiba; the Party held a perpetual majority
fouta	a length of fabric that men wrap around their waists, covering the body from navel to knee; here, an apron
gazuz	soda pop in Tunisian dialect
ghula	feminine form of *ghul*, Arabic for monster
gourbi	a shack or slum dwelling
hallouf	"pig" in North African dialect
harissa	a spicy red-pepper condiment widely used in Tunisian cooking
"Horyaa, karama, watanyaa..."	"Liberty, dignity, love of country..."
ib	indecent gesture or sinful act, depending on context
"Ihda chaabou wayman arada el hayyat, fala bouda an yastajiba al qadar."	from the celebrated verses of the Tunisian national poet, Abou El Kacem Chebbi, that make up the Tunisian national anthem: "If the people one day will to live / Destiny must then respond"
Khaldun, Ibn	born in 1332 in Tunis, Ibn Khaldun was a historian, philosopher, diplomat, and political figure; he is considered the father of modern sociology.

khobzistes	literally "breadwinners" — humble people who earn their livelihood simply and don't get involved in politics
kitab	book
kuffar	nonbelievers
"Marhaba bik fi Tounis, ya lilla Nadia!"	"Welcome to Tunis, Madame Nadia"
Rabbi yostor	God help us!
Réussite, La	French for "success"
safsari	a long length of silk or polyester fabric, depending on social class, that Tunisian women customarily use when they leave the house. The *safsari* covers the hair and the body, leaving only the face exposed.
Shahada	testimony of faith uttered by converts to Islam, and by Muslims in each of their five daily prayers.
shnua	Tunisian dialect expression meaning "what's up?" or "what is it," most often to indicate surprise or displeasure.
tawila	table
"Tounous horra horra... wanidham ala barra."	Tunisia will always be free; the regime will soon be gone"
UGTT	Union générale tunisienne du travail: Tunisian General Labour Union

...qot hazb el des- ..., yasqot jallad ..'ab!"	"Down with the Destourian Party; down with the hangman of the people!"
...ézoua	small pot with a long handle used for brewing Turkish coffee
zhar	Tunisian dialect term for luck
zoufris	originally "workers" in Tunisian dialect, now used to describe punks or rowdy young people

MONIA MAZIGH was born and raised in Tunisia and immigrated to Canada in 1991. She was catapulted onto the public stage in 2002 when her husband, Maher Arar, was deported to Syria where he was tortured and held without charge. She campaigned tirelessly for his release. Mazigh holds a PhD in finance from McGill University. She has published a memoir, *Hope and Despair*, and her novel, *Mirrors and Mirages*, was a finalist for the Trillium Book Award, in the original French.

International journalist and award-winning literary translator FRED A. REED is also a respected specialist on politics and religion in the Middle East. He has reported extensively on Middle Eastern affairs for *La Presse*, CBC Radio-Canada, and *Le Devoir*. A three-time winner of the Governor General's Literary Award for Translation, Reed has translated many works, including Monia Mazigh's debut novel, *Mirrors and Mirages*. He lives in Montreal.